"*The Seduction of Lord Stone* is romantic, emotional, sexy and funny. In fact, everything I have come to expect from Anna Campbell. I'm looking forward to reading the other Dashing Widows' stories." —*RakesandRascals.com*

"With her marvelous combination of humor and poignancy Anna Campbell writes in such a way that every story of hers has a special meaning and remains like a sentimental keepsake with those fortunate enough to read her work!" —*JeneratedReviews.com*

"*Lord Garson's Bride* is a well written and passionate story that touched my heart and sent my emotions on a rollercoaster ride. I particularly recommend this book for fans of convenient marriages, and those who enjoy seeing a deserving character find out that love is lovelier the second time around." —*Roses Are Blue Reviews*

"Campbell immediately hooks readers, then deftly reels them in with a spellbinding love story fueled by an addictive mixture of sharp wit, lush sensuality, and a wealth of well-delineated characters."—*Booklist, starred review, on A Scoundrel by Moonlight*

"With its superbly nuanced characters, impeccably crafted historical setting, and graceful writing shot through with scintillating wit, Campbell's latest lusciously sensual, flawlessly written historical Regency ... will have romance readers sighing happily with satisfaction."—*Booklist, Starred Review, on What a Duke Dares*

"Campbell makes the Regency period pop in the appealing third Sons of Sin novel. Romantic fireworks, the constraints of custom, and witty banter are combined in this sweet and successful story."—*Publishers Weekly on What a Duke Dares*

"Campbell is exceptionally talented, especially with plots that challenge the reader, and emotions and characters that are complex and memorable."—*Sarah Wendell, Smart Bitches Trashy Books, on A Rake's Midnight Kiss*

"A lovely, lovely book that will touch your heart and remind you why you read romance."—*Liz Carlyle, New York Times bestselling author on What a Duke Dares*

"Campbell holds readers captive with her highly intense, emotional, sizzling and dark romances. She instinctually knows how to play on her readers' fantasies to create a romantic, deep-sigh tale."—*RT Book Reviews, Top Pick, on Captive of Sin*

"Don't miss this novel - it speaks to the wild drama of the heart, creating a love story that really does transcend class."—*Eloisa James, New York Times bestselling author, on Tempt the Devil*

"*Seven Nights in A Rogue's Bed* is a lush, sensuous treat. I was enthralled from the first page to the last and still wanted more."—*Laura Lee Guhrke, New York Times bestselling author*

"No one does lovely, dark romance or lovely, dark heroes like Anna Campbell. I love her books."—*Sarah MacLean, New York Times bestselling author*

"It isn't just the sensuality she weaves into her story that makes Campbell a fan favorite, it's also her strong, three-dimensional characters, sharp dialogue and deft plotting. Campbell intuitively knows how to balance the key elements of the genre and give readers an irresistible, memorable read."—*RT Book Reviews, Top Pick, on Midnight's Wild Passion*

"Anna Campbell is an amazing, daring new voice in romance."—*Lorraine Heath, New York Times bestselling author*

"Ms. Campbell's gorgeous writing a true thing of beauty..."—*Joyfully Reviewed*

"She's the mistress of dark, sexy and brooding and takes us into the dens of iniquity with humor and class."—*Bookseller-Publisher Australia*

"Anna Campbell is a master at drawing a reader in from the very first page and keeping them captivated the whole book through. Ms. Campbell's books are all on my keeper shelf and *Midnight's Wild Passion* will join them proudly. *Midnight's Wild Passion* is a smoothly sensual delight that was a joy to read and I cannot wait to revisit Antonia and Nicholas's romance again."—*Joyfully Reviewed*

"Ms. Campbell gives us...the steamy sex scenes, a heroine whose backbone is pure steel and a stupendous tale of lust and love and you too cannot help but fall in love with this tantalizing novel."—*Coffee Time Romance*

"Anna Campbell offers us again, a lush, intimate, seductive read. I am in awe of the way she keeps the focus tight on the hero and heroine, almost achingly so. Nothing else really exists in this world, but the two main characters. Intimate, sensual story with a hero that will take your breath away."—*Historical Romance Books & More*

ALSO BY ANNA CAMPBELL

Claiming the Courtesan

Untouched

Tempt the Devil

Captive of Sin

My Reckless Surrender

Midnight's Wild Passion

The Sons of Sin series:

Seven Nights in a Rogue's Bed

Days of Rakes and Roses

A Rake's Midnight Kiss

What a Duke Dares

A Scoundrel by Moonlight

Three Proposals and a Scandal

The Dashing Widows:

The Seduction of Lord Stone

Tempting Mr. Townsend

Winning Lord West

Pursuing Lord Pascal

Charming Sir Charles

Catching Captain Nash

Lord Garson's Bride

The Lairds Most Likely:

The Laird's Willful Lass

The Laird's Christmas Kiss

The Highlander's Lost Lady

Christmas Stories:

The Winter Wife

Her Christmas Earl

A Pirate for Christmas

Mistletoe and the Major

A Match Made in Mistletoe

The Christmas Stranger

Other Books:

These Haunted Hearts

Stranded with the Scottish Earl

CATCHING CAPTAIN NASH

THE DASHING WIDOWS BOOK 6

ANNA CAMPBELL

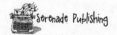
Serenade Publishing

ISBN: 978-0-6483987-8-3

Cover design: By Hang Le

Print editions published by Serenade Publishing
www.serenadepublishing.com

To Nicola Cornick, a truly excellent writer and a good friend

CHAPTER ONE

Nash House, Berkeley Square, London, October 1829

*T*he man stood in the shadows, watching the house across the square.

It was late, almost midnight, but the tall, white mansion was brightly lit, and lilting music from inside drifted across to him on the sharp autumn air. Carriages lined the square, waiting for the guests to make their way home after the party.

The night was bitterly cold, with a breeze that whistled around him and cut like a knife. His eyes never leaving the house, he huddled into his rough coat and stamped his booted feet to restore circulation.

He had a right to enter and join the fashionable throng, however unsuitably he was dressed. But something—diffidence, reluctance, perhaps even fear—made him hesitate before he stepped forward.

He'd rushed up to London the moment he disembarked at Gravesend. Now, shivering outside a house he hadn't seen in nearly five years, he couldn't bring himself to cross the threshold.

But he'd loitered so long in the empty square, he started to feel absurd. As if to signal it was time to reclaim his life, the music stopped. After a pause, he heard applause. Some celebration must take place inside.

Straightening, he strode ahead to the short flight of stairs. As he reached the open front door, he heard warm laughter and more applause from the back of the house.

He'd prepared to announce himself to a butler or footman, but it seemed even the servants deserted their posts to witness whatever took place here tonight.

Robert stepped into a familiar marble hall, bright with candlelight. The luxurious décor in Lord Stone's London home struck him like a punch to the solar plexus. Over the last years, for days on end, any light at all would have been a blessing. This shining gilt and glass overwhelmed his senses.

He paused to suck in an unsteady breath and find his balance. How ludicrous that he'd kept his courage—sometimes by a mere thread—through all his tribulations. Yet walking into this beautiful, much-loved house, he wanted to cry like an abandoned baby.

He followed the distant rumble of a deep voice. The high double doors to the ballroom, inlaid with twin family crests of crowned swans, stood open as if to welcome the prodigal son's return, but nobody turned to observe him come in.

The huge room was crowded. Everyone had their backs to the entrance and watched the people standing in front of the orchestra.

Robert was tall enough to look over the sea of heads. His eyes glanced across the group holding the floor. His brother Silas, his sister-in-law Caroline, his sister Amy. The famously handsome Lord Pascal. Another big brute of a fellow, whose name he couldn't immediately remember.

All his attention arrowed onto the woman standing beside Silas. His heart slammed against his ribs. His blood surged with possessiveness. Briefly the tears he'd fought in the hall rose again to blur his vision. He'd crossed oceans to find her, and now, by God, he had.

Feverishly he drank in the details of her appearance. Five years apart, and she looked just the same. Shining dark hair tied up in some folderol, although in his memory, it always cascaded around her bare white shoulders in ebony disarray.

Delicate and slender. When he'd first met her, he'd feared some misstep born of clumsy masculinity might mar her perfection. Only leaving her for the last time had he started to appreciate the strength she concealed beneath her beauty.

The rest of the room faded to nothing, while his hungry eyes fed on the sight of her. His heart swelled to fill his chest, making breathing impossible. He'd spent an eternity convinced he'd never see her again.

Yet here she was. And so miraculously unchanged.

How the devil had she stayed so unchanged? That flaring, dark beauty remained as vivid as his memories. While he felt like he'd aged a hundred years.

Still nobody looked back to see who ventured unannounced into this happy gathering. Because it was a happy gathering. Goodwill practically dripped from the elegant light green walls with their moldings of festive garlands and ribbons.

His disorientation faded enough for him to realize that Silas, Lord Stone, was giving a formal speech to his guests. Stupidly, Robert had noticed little beyond the lovely black-haired woman wearing peacock blue silk.

Silas's words hardly penetrated the waves of bewildered emotion engulfing him. Robert had always imagined that if this moment ever arrived, he'd be in transports of joy. But this felt too much like a confused dream to allow for anything as uncomplicated as mere happiness.

Then the dream turned dark and cold.

Disbelieving, he watched Silas take Morwenna's hand, gloved in dark blue to match her sumptuous gown, and offer it to the big cove.

Garson. That was his name. At last Robert remembered.

Rich as Croesus. Old friend of Silas's.

And he made sense of what until now had been little more than a muffled babble over the deafening roar of his heartbeat.

"I'm delighted to announce the betrothal of my dear sister-in-law Morwenna to one of the finest men I know. Hugh Rutherford, Baron Garson. Morwenna and Garson, I couldn't be happier for both of you. I wish you many years of joy ahead." Silas faced the crowd with a beaming smile. "Now it is my great pleasure to ask you all to raise your glasses in a toast to the happy couple."

"No..." But nobody heard Robert's low growl of denial.

Through a red haze, he watched Garson lift Morwenna's hand and place a kiss on the knuckles.

"No," he said more loudly.

This time, a few heads turned toward him. But he had no thought for other people.

Clumsily, on legs that felt as unwieldy as blocks of wood, he shoved his way forward. Every cell in his body burned to rip Garson's handsome head from those wide, straight shoulders. He hardly cared that he knocked aside the nation's most powerful men and their wives in his battle to reach the front. All he cared about was ending this abomination.

"No."

This time his strangled cry rose to reach his family. Silas, tall like him, frowned across at the disturbance, then turned as white as parchment and staggered back. His wife Caro was slower to notice, as was Amy. Morwenna, damn her, still stared entranced at the man who held her hand.

Robert stumbled to the front as a couple of brawny footmen rushed in his direction, clearly intent on ejecting this disreputable interloper.

Silas waved his hand to them and spoke in a choked voice. "Stop."

The footmen halted in their tracks, as the crowd receded to leave Robert standing in isolation. His chest was heaving, and that agonizing feeling of unreality compounded as he watched Morwenna step closer to Garson.

"Let her go," he said unsteadily to the big bastard. "She's not yours. She's mine."

At the sound of his voice, Morwenna stiffened, then turned in his direction in a swirl of rich blue. She ripped her hand away from Garson, but Robert was too far gone in rage and disbelief to find any satisfaction in that.

For one blazing moment, he read transcendent happiness in her face. Then the blue eyes, clear and changeable as the Cornish seas that lapped around her birthplace, dulled, and he saw unmistakable shame.

And dear Lord above, fear.

"Robert?" she whispered, although he heard his name as clearly as if she'd shouted.

"Of course," he said coldly.

To do his wife justice, she'd always been brave. While the blood drained from her face, leaving her like a ghost, she stood her ground before him and didn't fall into a faint.

No, it was his sister Amy who stared at him with glassy eyes, then collapsed into the arms of the golden-haired Adonis beside her.

CHAPTER TWO

The room receded from Morwenna in an alarming rush, and the loud buzz of curiosity and concern that rose from the crowd reached her from a long way away. The only real thing in the room was her husband's face.

His beloved face.

But so changed. When she looked into that face that had filled her dreams, she didn't see the light-hearted, laughing man she'd married, but a stranger.

Her first, dazed glance told her that he'd been through hell on earth to reach her. He looked pale and ill, with the skin stretched tight over his cheekbones. A long scar divided his cheek from temple to jaw. She flinched as she imagined a sword slicing down to inflict that cruel cut. An inch higher, and he'd have lost an eye.

Yet he remained the most compelling man she'd

ever seen. Even worn and hurt and bristling with hostility.

Those striking features had been carved on her heart from the moment six years ago, when she'd first seen him in the Truro assembly rooms. He was dark, dark enough to be a Cornishman, with the same snapping black eyes as his sister Helena.

Robert had been tall and elegant when they met, dashing in his naval uniform. Just promoted to captain, the youngest in the navy, a mark of his brilliance as a navigator, and his heroic deeds along the Barbary Coast.

All the Truro girls were mad for him, but he'd had eyes only for the local belle, Morwenna St. Leger. Their courtship had been quick and passionate. It had been a near thing that she'd arrived in her marriage bed a virgin.

But life as a sailor's wife meant long stretches alone. In their year together, they spent mere weeks under one roof. Enough time for Robert to leave her carrying their daughter Kerenza, when he sailed away to map the coast of South America, the voyage from which he'd never returned.

Morwenna had spent the years since lost in a fog of grief, consoled only by her love for her daughter and the kindness of Robert's grand relations. The brother of a peer had been a catch for a girl from an obscure family and an isolated, hard-scrabble corner of the kingdom. Except none of the Nashes had been grand at all. And through their profound sorrow, they'd found room for Robert's bride, and later Robert's pretty, quirky, stubborn daughter. It was both a comfort and an excruciating reminder of her loss that Kerenza could be nobody else's daughter but Robert Nash's.

Morwenna's immediate reaction was to fling herself into his arms. She could hardly believe this miracle. The missing, bleeding half of her heart was at last restored to her. She'd felt barely alive since that devastating day when his lieutenant came to Woodley Park with news that Captain Robert Nash, R.N., was dead. He'd gone overboard after being shot in an engagement with pirates in the South Atlantic.

Then she remembered that Robert had returned to find her pledging herself to another man.

She forced air into starved lungs. She locked her knees against collapsing and struggled to clear her head. A few feet away, Pascal tried to revive his wife, Robert's sister Amy.

Of course Robert wouldn't know about Amy's recent marriage. With the force of a blow, she realized that it was likely Robert didn't know he had a child.

The room whirled around her. Reaching to hold onto something, anything, she curled her hand over Lord Garson's arm.

Then was sorry she had when she saw Robert's eyes flare with temper. The man she'd married had been slow to anger and quick to forgive. She could already tell this formidable creature wasn't nearly so tolerant.

She snatched her hand away and blushed with guilt, even as she reminded herself she'd done nothing wrong. But when she met condemning black eyes, any small power that reassurance had held drained away to nothing.

Around them, a deathly hush had fallen. Logic told Morwenna that the silence lasted a few seconds, but she felt like she tumbled into an endless, soundless cavern, where nothing existed beyond Robert's burning, angry glare.

Silas, thank God, ended the ghastly stasis.

"Robert...Robert, old man..." His broken words vibrated with joy. He strode forward and hauled his brother into a fervent embrace.

Morwenna watched Robert stiffen as if expecting violence. Then her heart cramped with wordless compassion when he hesitantly slid his arms around his brother's back.

Where on earth had Robert been all this time? Everyone on his ship had seen him dragged under the waves, and he hadn't resurfaced. She knew this was true because she and Silas had tracked down all the surviving crew, from the cabin boy to the first lieutenant. Anyone who might have offered a shred of hope that the man she loved still lived.

Because if he didn't live, how could she continue in a world without him? Even as she grew large with his child inside her.

She'd taken years to accept that Robert really was

dead. He'd seemed too vital and powerful to fall victim to common mortality.

It turned out that she'd been right to doubt his demise. Even now, when he glowered at her like he hated her, her soul expanded to fill her for the first time since he'd gone.

He was alive. He was alive.

That was all that mattered. He might never speak another kind word to her, but he breathed the same air she did.

She sucked in another breath, and this time had no trouble standing on her own two feet. And with the action, her reeling shock receded a little and she became aware of her surroundings. Pascal had carried Amy to a chair, but she looked wan and shaky. Brief, distant curiosity sparked in Morwenna's mind. Was her sister-in-law with child?

Caro was crying, unashamed tears pouring down her lovely face. "If only Helena was here," she said in a thick voice.

Around her, Morwenna heard the gale of whispers. The curiosity. The hint of spiteful enjoyment. She saw the bright, malicious glances directed at her, and Lord Garson beside her.

With horror, she recalled the man she'd agreed to marry next Christmas. She turned to Garson, then almost wished she hadn't.

He watched her with that steady gaze that had

become so familiar over recent months. But at last she recognized the depth of love behind his eyes.

Remorse stabbed her. She'd known he cared about her. Of course, she did. But only now when there could be nothing more between them did she see that he loved her perhaps almost as much as she loved Robert.

Morwenna realized that in accepting his proposal out of pure self-interest, she'd done him a disservice. She'd been honest enough to tell him she still loved her husband. But as their eyes met, she read his dashed hopes that time would loosen Robert's hold on her.

His level, gray gaze told her something else. He now understood that even without Robert's return, no man had ever had a chance of gaining her heart.

And the knowledge cut him to the bone.

Morwenna wanted to say she was sorry—and she was —but her regret was a tiny shadow in the huge, spinning universe of gratitude that Robert had come back to her.

Despite everything, she found a moment's astonished admiration when Garson bowed and stepped back. It was an acknowledgment that in this particular competition, there could only be one winner.

And it wasn't him.

All of this filled the time it took Silas and Robert to shift apart.

"How the devil has this happened?" Silas's voice still cracked with emotion. "The Admiralty gave us no hope that you'd survived."

Robert shook his head, as Pascal tore himself from Amy's side. "Silas, I think the family should hear this story first, before it becomes generally known."

Silas looked around, and Morwenna saw that he'd forgotten the room full of people. He'd only seen his brother, returned from the dead. "Yes. Of course."

After nodding to the servants to take their places, Pascal raised his voice. "My friends, you came here tonight to witness a joyous event. And so you have, if not the one you expected. We beg your indulgence in giving us a little privacy to welcome Captain Nash back to his home and family and find out the story behind his return."

People began moving toward the entrance. Without looking, Silas reached out to find Caro's hand. She, with that unspoken communication built over eight years of marriage, was already there at his side.

Another pang struck Morwenna. Before he left, she and Robert had been passionate lovers, but close to strangers in most other ways. If fate had been kinder, they should by now have formed the same bond as Silas and Caro.

She and her husband had missed out on so much. Was it too late to find each other again?

Or was the break irreparable?

Studying this stern man in his rough sailor's clothes, she couldn't feel confident of a happy ending. Misery tightened her belly, and she sagged where she stood.

Caro came to take Morwenna's arm. "Are you all right?"

She nodded, although she was far from sure. A torrent of words pressed against her trembling lips, but her husband's closed expression kept her silent.

"Rob, I didn't think I'd ever see you again." Amy stood on shaky legs and stumbled across to hug her brother. "I'm so happy that you're alive."

The paralysis that had gripped everyone gradually eased. The shock that had felt like horror, but was really astounded, incomprehensible elation, now softened to something a little more bearable.

Robert even seemed less awkward with human contact as he bent to hug his sister. In Silas's embrace, he'd looked ready to fight or run. The man Morwenna had married had always worn a smile. This man hadn't smiled once, although surely he must be glad to be back.

And he'd given no sign that he remembered his wife with any special fondness. No sign except that furious cry denying Garson's claim on her.

Now those fathomless eyes met hers as he leaned over a sobbing Amy. Morwenna caught a flash of something that could be vulnerability. He looked away before she could be sure. But this was the first hint that the man she'd married might lurk somewhere inside this forbidding stranger.

"Robert, let me tell you..." she said in a croak that faded to nothing. Appeal? Apology? Welcome? She wasn't sure herself. But he didn't hear her over the hubbub in the room.

The crowd slowly dispersed. The men clapped Robert and Silas on the back in congratulations, while the women smiled. Or if they were sentimental, dabbed their eyes with lace handkerchiefs. A few curious souls lingered as the ranks thinned, hoping for some gossip to take away. But Silas and his staff were polite but relentless in clearing the house.

If those who appreciated a scandal wished to witness a brawl between the newly resurrected husband and the recently deposed fiancé, they would have been doomed to disappointment.

"Morwenna, can I do anything to help?" Garson turned to her with the consideration she'd learned to appreciate over the last months.

Automatically she presented her hand, and he bowed over it. Since she'd accepted his offer of marriage, he usually kissed her fingers. Not tonight.

"You're very kind," she said, and meant it. His face expressed only concern for her. Any darker feelings remained masked. "Especially when..."

His faint smile was more proof of his gallantry. "Clearly we weren't meant to be." He glanced across to where Amy smiled up at Robert with unadulterated happiness.

How Morwenna envied Robert's family's uncomplicated reaction to his return. She wanted to smile and laugh and cheer, too, but she couldn't shake off her memory of that accusing glare when he saw her holding Garson's hand. "Yes, but…"

Garson stopped her, which was a mercy, as she had no idea what she meant to say. "I'm glad for your sake he's back."

A muscle jerked in his cheek, a hint of the effort it took to say that.

"Thank you." She felt Robert watching her again, then she realized Garson still held her hand. She withdrew, praying she didn't look as guilty as she felt.

"It's best if I go. Send word if you need me."

"I will." Except the sad truth was that now the man she loved was here, Garson, for all his many marvelous qualities, had become irrelevant.

Love was a ruthless master.

He bowed again and left, the last guest to go.

She supposed she could approach Robert, insist on taking her place beside him. She was his wife, after all. But something about his rigid stance kept her marooned where she was. She'd barely shifted from where she'd stood when Silas had made the heartfelt speech about welcoming his good friend Lord Garson into the family. If Caro hadn't been holding her arm, she'd have felt alone indeed.

Morwenna had always imagined that if the unbelievable happened and Robert came back, she'd launch herself into his arms without a second thought. But Robert in her fantasies had been the charmer she'd married. An invisible wall surrounded this austere revenant. At least as far as his wife was concerned.

Which didn't stop her longing to touch him to prove he was real, the way someone perishing of thirst burned for a drop of water.

Through the ocean of conflicting emotions engulfing her, she drank in the details of his appearance. His hair was too long, and ragged with a bad cut. Whiskers shadowed his jaw. He'd always had a vigorous beard.

"This calls for a celebration indeed." Silas signaled to the butler. "Champagne, Hunter."

Ignoring her half-hearted resistance, Caro drew Morwenna forward. Robert showed no reaction to his wife coming to stand a foot away from him. A chill ran up her spine, and she shivered.

Caro noticed and mouthed the word "courage." Then she released Morwenna and laid a hand on Silas's arm. "Perhaps we should save our carousing until tomorrow, darling. This has been the most wonderful night, and we all have so much to find out. But it's late, and Robert looks ready to drop where he stands."

"But..." Amy protested, then subsided into silence under Caro's repressive look.

"I'll bring you here for breakfast, sweetheart," Pascal said. "You won't miss anything, I promise."

"If I must wait, I must," Amy said grudgingly. She gave Robert another hug, not appearing to note his tepid response. "Good night, Rob. I'm so glad you're back."

Silas turned to the butler. "Hunter, forget the champagne. Instead, please prepare a room for Captain Nash."

Robert frowned at his brother. Was Morwenna the only person attuned to the subtle parade of emotions on his face? Had anyone else seen the way those tense, straight shoulders under their ill-fitting coat had eased when Caro suggested leaving explanations until the morning?

"The blue chamber," Caro said.

Robert swallowed, then spoke. He'd been taciturn in the extreme since coming in. Another change from his former self. "No."

"You'd prefer a different room? Or have you already arranged lodgings?" Silas asked. "Please say you'll sleep here. Otherwise I'll wake up and decide I dreamed that you're back."

Robert spoke again, slowly as though each word emerged after he'd dredged it out of the depths. "My place is with my wife."

Morwenna stiffened and stared at him in consternation. Another shiver rippled through her, this one made up of sheer alarm. Heaven help her. Did he mean to chastise her tonight, before she'd had a chance to come to terms with his arrival? She already felt on the verge of shattering. Defending herself to an angry husband asked too much of her right now.

Caro cast Morwenna a concerned glance. "Robert, perhaps it might be better if…"

Stubbornly Robert shook his coal-black head. "No."

Silas sent her a worried look. "Morwenna?"

Of course he was worried about her. Nobody knew better than he how she'd grieved. He'd been delighted when she'd accepted Sally, Lady Norwood's invitation to come to London this season to rejoin society and play a Dashing Widow. He'd never been insensitive enough to tell her to take up her life again, but his pleasure in her social success was clear. As clear as his approval of her engagement to Garson.

"Of course." She forced leaden legs to bring her closer to Robert. She'd never been more aware of how little time she and her husband had spent alone together, and the abyss now yawning between them.

Robert's expression didn't change, and he didn't look at her. What happened now? Should she take his arm and show him the way to her room? Did he want her to touch him? She'd quickly guessed that during his absence, he'd become uncomfortable with physical contact.

His hand, tanned, scarred and unfamiliar, snaked out to curl around her wrist. The first time he'd touched her in five years.

Even through her satin glove, she felt the heat. When she jumped, he cast her a narrow-eyed look and tightened his grip. For so long, she'd ached for his touch, but this ruthless hold made her feel like a dog on a tight leash.

"We'll see you at breakfast," Caro said with an unconvincing attempt at brightness. "Robert, please say you'll tell us in the morning what happened to you. We're agog to hear it."

"Give the man a chance to catch his breath, my love." Silas's smile softened the reproof.

She sent him an unimpressed glance. "You're as eager to hear as I am."

He shrugged and slid his arm around his wife's waist. "Of course I am."

Once the banter would have amused Robert, but tonight he hardly seemed to hear it. Instead his grip on Morwenna's arm firmed, until she feared he'd leave a bruise.

On his way out, Silas paused beside his brother and squeezed his shoulder. "We've missed you so damned much."

Without speaking, Robert nodded. Then far too quickly for her to decide on a strategy for handling this daunting stranger, Morwenna was alone with her husband.

"I need to..." she began, not sure what she wanted to say, but frantic to bridge this chasm.

He shook his head again. "Not here. Upstairs."

She bit the inside of her cheek to stop bursting into tears. With every breath, she'd wanted him back. Now, against all the odds, he was here.

Yet she was tongue-tied and awkward and miserable. Her stomach churned with relief and gratitude and terror—and disbelief that he was here at all. She gulped back the rising queasiness and tried again. "I'm glad you're back, too."

Stale, weak, inadequate words for the way her heart had leaped to life at the sound of his deep voice when he'd burst through the crowd.

He turned his head to study her. She couldn't read his expression, when once she'd felt she knew his every thought. "Upstairs."

She told herself that she could survive this. After all this time without him, she could survive anything. Even his return.

Straightening her spine, she guided him to the base of the magnificent marble staircase rising to the upper floors. With every step, her heart beat out the stark truth that formed her only defense against crippling fear.

"He's alive. He's alive. Nothing else matters a tinker's damn."

CHAPTER THREE

*M*orwenna brought her husband upstairs to the bedroom she'd slept in for the last few months. When she'd first come to London, she'd lived with Sally, Lady Norwood, as part of their pact to play Dashing Widows, women of independent spirit who had fun and dazzled society. But Sally had recently married Sir Charles Kinglake, and was touring Italy on her wedding trip. Morwenna desperately wished Sally was here in London—she had a suspicion she might need a friend before everything was settled with Robert.

Her maid put aside the mending to greet her mistress with a curtsy and quickly hidden surprise at a man's presence in this, until now, purely feminine territory.

Well, the girl would find out plenty once she went down to the servants' hall. Morwenna had been in

Town long enough to know that Robert's return would be the subject of conversation from cellars to attics in every house in Mayfair.

Let them talk. She didn't care. Her love was alive.

Right now, Robert wouldn't want an audience, so she sent the girl away. Although heaven knew how she'd get out of this gown without help.

Once they were alone, Robert didn't shift from the threshold. The hand on her wrist was trembling. Tiredness? Anger? Some mysterious illness?

Morwenna didn't know. And she didn't feel she could ask this stranger, who wasn't entirely a stranger.

Because his touch made her burn the way she hadn't burned in five years. And his scent teased dormant senses back to tingling life. The shabby coat reeked of salt and old fish, but beneath it, even after so long, she knew that warm, male smell. At an animal level, her body immediately recognized this man as her mate.

She tipped her head to study him. He seemed dazed, and at last she saw his bone-deep weariness. Caro was right. He looked ready to collapse from exhaustion.

With a soft sound of distress, she reached to touch his face. "Oh, my dear," she whispered, hating how he flinched away. "Tell me what you want."

He sucked in a shuddering breath. By now, his trembling was visible. She expected another monosyllabic response, but he shot her a sharp look and said, "Now, there's a question."

She frowned, wishing she was clever like the Nashes, clever enough to know how to heal him. Before she could summon an answer, he pulled away, pressing his hand to the doorframe in a silent admission that he couldn't stand unsupported. Morwenna began to reach for him again, until she recalled how he'd shied away from her.

"You know, I should leave you." He started to turn toward the corridor. "I'll see you in the morning."

To her surprise, she found herself saying, "No, stay."

She found the courage to take his arm. He went rigid as a gatepost under her hold, apart from that awful trembling. She had no idea what he'd been through, but she knew enough to understand that whatever had happened to him left him stretched to the absolute limit.

He didn't look at her. "I'm not fit company tonight."

She made a disgusted sound. "I'm your wife. You don't have to be company." She almost spat out the last word.

He leveled a flat gaze on her. "I wasn't sure you remembered you were my wife."

A spurt of temper briefly overcame her lingering guilt. "It's been five years, Robert, and everyone was certain you were dead."

He looked startled, as well he might. So far, she'd been a bit of a mouse in the face of his antipathy.

"I remembered you every moment," he said harshly.

And I remembered you, my love.

She didn't say it. Now wasn't the time for declarations of love. Although she was heartened to hear that he'd never stopped thinking of her. "There are things you need to know."

Those marked black brows contracted in a scowl, and a muscle jerked in his cheek. "Let's leave the confessions until tomorrow, Morwenna."

This was the first time he'd spoken her name since his return. She wished those straight white teeth didn't bite it off like something unpleasant.

It was her turn to frown as she assessed what he'd said. She'd referred to Kerenza, not to any misbehavior in his absence, although he must wonder about her engagement to Garson.

"I wasn't..." she began, but he silenced her with a wave of his hand.

"I'm sorry," he said, without sounding particularly apologetic. "I have no right to carp. You'd had confirmation of my death."

"You have the rights of a husband," she said.

His lips twisted, but not in a smile. "A dead husband has no rights."

"Robert..."

He stepped out of her hold and at once, she missed the contact, despite the tension rising between them. "I should have left you alone tonight."

She met his stare, again wishing she was sure of herself with him. One thing she was sure of—she'd never seen a man look so lonely. Despite the way his family had welcomed him, isolation clung to him like an icy shroud. "Do you want to go?"

He didn't reply, but the quickly concealed hunger in his eyes was answer enough. Not the hunger of desire, but something else. She could only think it was a hunger for warmth and human contact.

Her lips tightened. His pride was familiar. When she'd first come to know him, his pride had surprised her. After all, he was accounted the most agreeable of fellows and always brightened any gathering.

But a core of steel lurked beneath the geniality. That core of steel had helped him rise through the naval ranks with unprecedented speed. She also suspected that core of steel had kept him alive through whatever torments he'd endured.

Which didn't stop her from wanting to slap him for the way he currently held onto his foolish masculine pride. But at least he became less a stranger with every minute.

Downstairs, this hollow-eyed wanderer had revealed little trace of the man she'd married. Now her confidence revived when she saw that despite time, distance and untold suffering, her Robert existed in there somewhere.

"Then for heaven's sake, stop playing the martyr and come into the room," she said with asperity. Still, she was wise enough to move fully inside and leave him space to make his decision.

After a second, he edged through the doorway. She

sucked in a relieved breath. She felt like she coaxed a wild creature close enough to eat from her hand. A game of advance and retreat, requiring endless patience and calm.

Robert came to a halt in the center of the pretty, feminine room with its pink silk curtains and graceful furniture. He looked as out of place as a stevedore in Almack's.

Warily he surveyed his surroundings, until his eyes met his reflection in a cheval mirror. He winced and looked away. "You must think me a complete vagabond."

He spoke more easily now, she was grateful to hear. Each word no longer seemed to hurt. In the ballroom, she'd noticed that he'd relaxed a tad as the crowd left.

She shrugged, and to save herself from falling all over him in tearful gratitude for his return, she sat in front of her dressing table and began dismantling the elaborate hairstyle she'd worn for the betrothal party. Some instinct warned her that too much emotion would threaten Robert's barely held control. And he was clinging to his control as if it was his last lifeline. More pride.

"I'm guessing you came straight from a ship." It was an effort to speak evenly, but those same instincts told her that he'd prefer some semblance of normality to the high drama his return warranted.

He rewarded her circumspection with the longest sentences he'd yet managed. "Yes, we docked this evening. I probably should have waited to make sure I looked marginally civilized before I arrived."

She stared into the mirror, but really she saw nothing. Her hands continued their busy work without her needing to pay attention. "No, you shouldn't."

He moved across to the window and pushed aside the drawn curtains. The clear night had turned to rain. The sound of raindrops splattering against the windows filled the awkward silence.

It was so long since she'd had a man in her bedroom. Had Robert's presence always been so restless, stirring up currents of disquiet with every breath? She couldn't help thinking of a lion pacing its cage. Was this lion going to turn and devour her?

"Do you want me to tell you where I've been?" he asked, without looking back at her.

Curiosity clawed at her, ferocious as the lion she'd likened him to. But audible reluctance had weighted his question. "Of course I do. But we promised to wait until tomorrow."

He turned to her, and she was surprised to catch a glimpse of grim humor in his eyes, even if that long mouth remained unsmiling. "You're a wife in a thousand."

She wasn't naive enough to take his remark as an unalloyed compliment. But at least he was talking to her now. "Why don't you take off your coat?" she said calmly, beginning to brush her thick, black hair out before she braided it.

"I've been living in rough shipboard conditions for weeks. I'm not dressed like a gentleman."

She made herself continue the steady downward stroke of the brush through hair as straight as a ruler. With a hungry expression that was becoming familiar, his attention focused on the everyday action.

"I'm sure I'll survive the sight of you in your shirt-sleeves," she said drily. With every second, the bed behind him loomed larger and larger in her mind. Not to mention the things they needed to do before they shared it. Undressing for one. "I'm surprised a footman didn't take your coat when you came into the house."

He shrugged off the coat with a reluctance she could read and laid it over one of the brocade armchairs near the roaring fire. It looked as out of place there as Robert looked out of place in this room.

"There were no servants at the door. They'd all gone inside to witness your betrothal announcement." He paused, folding his arms over the threadbare linen shirt that covered his chest. "Did you say something?"

"Just a knot," she said sweetly, although a gasp of annoyance had escaped her. She could imagine he wasn't best pleased to find her promising herself to another man, but her reasons had been sound. Someday she'd have to make him understand. But not tonight when they were both so on edge.

"I told you I'm not dressed for a lady's boudoir."

"You'll do," she said, wanting to tell him she didn't

care what he wore. She only cared that he was here
with her.

But while at last they were almost communicating,
she trembled on the brink of the chasm still gaping
between them.

She bit her lip and struggled to hold onto her
spurious serenity. It was difficult now she saw him
without the voluminous coat. He'd always been lean,
but the man before her was thin almost to emaciation.
He wore loose sailor's trousers in faded black, held up
by a thick leather belt with a tarnished buckle, and
heavy boots. She couldn't help remembering the
Robert she'd first met, who had been so dashing and
spruce in his immaculate naval uniform.

"The ship that picked me up was a whaler." As he
turned his head, the candlelight caught the shiny skin
of the scar marking his cheek. "No buttons and brass
anywhere."

The urge rose to find out more, but she beat it back.
She'd promised to wait, to save him having to live
through his ordeal twice when he spoke to the family
tomorrow. Because even without hearing details, she
could see he'd been through experiences harsh enough
to strip all the polish from a man's soul. "I can live
without buttons and brass."

I can't live without you.

Even when he was so wounded and wary, that was
true. She set down her brush and went on. "Would you

like anything to eat or drink? I could ring for something."

Good heavens, right now he looked like he needed a month of four square meals a day.

"No, thank you." He sank into another of those ridiculously feminine chairs and bent to take off his boots. The intimacy of the mundane act knocked the breath from her, although of course the moment he'd said he was coming upstairs, she'd understood that they'd share a bed. After all, there was only one bed in the room.

With unsteady fingers, she started to braid her hair.

He looked up from unlacing his boots and shot her a sharp glance. "No."

Her fingers stilled, as her eyes met his in the glass. Was the monosyllabic man who'd come into the ballroom back again? "No?"

One of his scarred hands gestured in her direction. "Your hair. Don't..."

"Plait it?"

"Please."

Oh, dear. That was a statement of intent, if she'd ever heard one.

Ridiculous to feel nervous, but trepidation settled like a boulder in her stomach. She'd desperately missed the Robert she'd married, wanted him back in her bed. But this man, despite occasional glimmers of familiarity, remained very much an unknown quantity.

His touch had always set her alight. She'd starved

for it since he'd gone away. But so much remained unresolved. While she owed him her duty as his wife, was it too much to ask him to wait?

She gulped in a mouthful of air and made herself nod. "Very well."

"Thank you." He rose on bare feet and prowled up behind her.

Without turning, she watched his approach in the mirror. Her stomach seethed with nerves. The skin prickled across her shoulders as she braced for contact.

He stared down at her as he loomed up, so she couldn't see his eyes. He paused, and her skin tightened in anticipation that she couldn't describe as wholly fearful or wholly eager.

Did he mean to kiss her? Sweep her up into his arms and into the bed? Then prove himself her husband in the most basic way?

But he merely lifted a tress of black hair and let it drift down through his fingers.

Now she could read the expression on his face.

More hunger.

He mightn't like her anymore. But after this, she couldn't doubt that he wanted her.

She gave a visible shiver and placed a hand over her churning stomach.

After a charged silence, he stepped away, allowing her space to rise on shaky legs. There was a tall screen set up near the fire. She'd never imagined feeling shy with the man who had shown her that her body was made for pleasure and love. But right now, nothing short of a pistol to the head could make her undress in front of him.

Like the frightened mouse she so despised, Morwenna snatched up the nightdress spread over the bed and scuttled behind the screen. There she slumped onto a padded stool and stared blindly into space.

It took her a shaming amount of time to find the heart to remove slippers and stockings. She even managed to take off her drawers and petticoats.

Her skin itched with awareness, although the room outside was so quiet that she could almost believe she was alone. But she was vividly conscious that her husband could hear every rustle from behind the screen.

"Blast..." she muttered.

"What is it?" a deep voice inquired from much closer than where she'd left him.

She was blushing like fire. Absurd, when they'd been naked together so many times. "I can't unlace my gown."

He appeared around the side of the screen. "Let me help."

She wanted to say no. But she'd look an utter fool going to bed in her finery. She lifted her slippery fall of hair out of the way and presented her back. "Thank you."

He'd done this for her before, of course. In those

heady, too brief days after their wedding. When she'd imagined a lifetime as Robert Nash's wife.

But still she jumped when his fingers brushed her nape. A sizzle of heat rippled down her spine, and her stomach lurched.

He began to tug at the fastenings with a clumsiness she didn't remember, and she realized that he was trembling again. She was so preternaturally aware of his closeness, she felt every faint hesitation in his fingers.

When it seemed to take him forever to finish, the breath snagged in her throat. She was seeing colored lights in front of her eyes before she remembered to take another breath.

Then she realized Robert was holding his breath, too.

That salty smell was rich in her nostrils, mingled with the underlying spice that was his alone. She'd never been so conscious of his height and power, even when she'd come to his bed as a virgin bride.

After about a hundred years, he reached her waist and briefly rested his hands on her hips. Despite her uncertainty, she had to resist the wanton urge to bump backward until her buttocks met his groin.

He'd taken her from behind several times. The memory was sharp in her mind. Since he'd been gone, she'd relived over and over everything they'd done together in their small house in Portsmouth.

The urgency to feel him invade her body became

overwhelming. She wasn't sure what she thought of this man who returned to her from his watery grave. But her body gave no heed to her mind's havering. Her body only knew that after a long famine, pleasure beckoned at last.

After a mere second, he released her. She made herself straighten, preparatory to stepping away, when she felt a tug on the laces of her stays.

A soft whoosh of breath escaped her. This was like torture.

This time his touch was sure, and she soon felt her corset sag. She reached up to clutch her bodice, before it slipped down to disgrace modesty. Although modesty was surely out of place when she stood before her husband.

For another bristling second, he remained behind her. Close enough to touch her. But not touching her.

She felt like she hung suspended over a precipice.

Morwenna quivered as she imagined those large hands, more disturbing than before with their scars and calluses, flattening over her breasts and hauling her back into his body. Starting to sway, she bit her lip and shut her eyes.

She sagged like her unlaced corset when he moved back. "All set?"

The crack in his voice hinted that unlacing her had been as fraught for him as for her. But that knowledge was more threat than reassurance.

"Th-thank you," she forced out.

She turned to look at him, but he'd left her alone behind the screen. Had he always moved so quietly? She shivered again. She had no idea what Robert was thinking, beyond the fact that despite his attempts to hide it, he hadn't stopped wanting her.

Oh, dear. She was so keyed up, she was likely to snap into pieces before the night was over. In a rush, she flung off her clothes and had a quick wash, hating the way the touch of her hand made her imagine other, harder hands stroking her skin.

Tonight sensuality edged everything she did. The brush of the sponge across her breasts with their brazenly tight pink nipples. Worse, washing between her legs. It was as if she'd been asleep for five years and only now awoke.

Once she'd pulled her filmy nightdress over her head, she loitered far too long behind the screen. She felt...bashful. Silly as it was to admit, when she'd been married for six years. A woman of twenty-six with a child shouldn't feel like an untried girl.

Still, she required a mammoth amount of will to step into the open.

"Oh," she said, struck as inarticulate as Robert had been downstairs.

He was sitting up in the bed, bare-chested, with the blankets pulled to his waist. Was he naked? With another of those dizzying lurches in her stomach, she supposed he must be.

"Come to bed," he said softly, and her blush rose again.

"I'll just blow out the candles," she said huskily.

But as she moved around the room, she couldn't forget what she'd seen when she looked at his torso. The sharply delineated ribs and collarbones. The scars marring arms and chest. Especially the long, angry slash stretching from his shoulder across his chest.

She'd known he'd suffered. But clearly she hadn't started to comprehend all he'd been through.

Once the room was dark, Morwenna paused in the shadows, shifting from foot to foot and mustering the nerve to go to the man she loved. She'd spent years yearning for this moment, convinced it would never come.

Yet now the time, astonishingly, miraculously, arrived. And she was an addled mixture of terror and longing.

Purely to delay joining Robert in that big bed, she stoked the fire to a roaring blaze. Then, sick of playing the sniveling coward, she swallowed, squared her shoulders under the silk nightdress, and stepped forward to slip beneath the covers.

She sat up against the pillows beside him, wondering again if he meant to seize her and place his claim on her. But he remained unmoving, staring out into the room, and keeping a good foot of space between them.

She waited for him to say something, explain his

intentions. Her heart careered into a gallop, and her skin tightened as she prepared to accept his advances.

The mad fact was that she'd wanted this so long, yet now felt completely unready. Her throat was so constricted, she was convinced she couldn't speak to save herself.

The silence extended and extended. Growing heavier with every second.

Still he didn't touch her.

Eventually the strains of the day began to tell. Morwenna had steeled herself to face this engagement party for weeks, long before Garson had formally declared himself. She'd known that she'd say yes to him. It was past time for her to take up a new life, instead of merely existing like a wraith trapped in a prison of grief.

But it had been so hard to take that step toward a new future.

She'd known Robert was dead, had finally accepted it in her mind. But her stubborn, loving heart had fought against taking another husband. Even though Garson was a good man, and she was lucky to have won his love.

So tonight's shocks had come hard upon weeks of tormented soul-searching and sleeplessness.

She'd have wagered everything she owned on not sleeping a wink. But her heavy lids drooped, and she found herself sliding down in the bed.

"Good night, Morwenna," Robert said softly, after what felt like hours.

"Good night," she mumbled back. And just on the verge of sleep, "I'm so happy you're back, Robert."

If he replied, she didn't hear him.

CHAPTER FOUR

*R*obert lay on his back beside his wife, wide awake and burning.

He'd spent long, lonely years hungering for just this. The comforts of home. The warmth of family. Above all, Morwenna, whose presence had fed his soul from the first time he saw her.

But reality turned out to be a horribly distorted version of the visions that had sustained him.

Seeing his family again had been wonderful, of course it was. But their open affection and joy had made his skin crawl. He wasn't used to dealing with crowds of people yet, despite eight weeks on the whaler that had rescued him. Those rough Norwegian sailors had largely left him alone, once they met his immediate physical needs for food and clothing, and once they'd done their best to patch up his wounds. The language barrier and also the code of hard men who faced danger every day of their lives had preserved Robert's privacy.

Entering that packed room downstairs had tied his gut in knots.

Now he stretched stiff—in all senses of the word—and wakeful on a soft feather mattress and the finest linen sheets. And his body, accustomed to a hard wooden pallet and freezing cold and damp, couldn't adjust to the change. He was dead tired, so exhausted every muscle ached, yet he couldn't sleep.

Nor could he stop stewing about the woman curled into a ball on the edge of the mattress, as though even in sleep, she could hardly bear his nearness.

His wife, who had told him there were things he needed to know. Did those "things" include a love affair with the man she'd planned to marry?

Dear God, perhaps she'd taken more than one lover. After all, he'd been gone a long time, and nobody knew better than Robert what a passionate creature Morwenna was.

Savage masculine rage settled in his belly, even as he admitted he was unfair. While his animal self might want the woman he loved to swear a vow of eternal chastity in her widowhood, the civilized man who still existed—just!—knew he was acting like a bear.

That civilized man told him he should be glad she'd gone on to find new happiness.

That civilized man could go to hell.

Whatever evil it spoke of him, he couldn't get over

believing Morwenna was his forever. On this side of heaven or the next. And be damned if he'd tolerate her making sheep's eyes at another man.

He wanted her like the devil. That was no surprise. He'd wanted her naked and in his bed since the first time he saw her at that woefully provincial assembly in Truro.

But he'd imagined on his homecoming, gratitude and sentiment would outweigh desire. In his captivity, he hadn't known a woman's touch, and for most of that time, he'd borne his celibacy with reasonable patience.

That wasn't the case right now. Celibacy in his wife's presence itched like the devil. Morwenna was lucky he hadn't pushed her down in front of that glittering crowd downstairs and claimed his rights. Just after he stuck a knife into that much admired gentleman, Lord Garson, so the bastard never again poached on Robert's dominion.

Lying beside her now, he barely contained his urge to tup her.

Which made him feel like a barbarian.

He hadn't missed the fear in her eyes when she'd looked at him. Fear and guilt. She'd trembled when he'd touched her, and almost collapsed with terror when he'd helped her with her dress. By the dickens, that had been a test of his willpower.

Perhaps she was right to be afraid. He didn't trust himself to touch her.

Robert closed his eyes, praying for oblivion. He

struggled not to brood upon whose bed Morwenna had shared while her husband starved in a rancid pit.

Tonight life had granted him everything he'd wished for during his exile. Years when he'd been convinced he'd never see England or the people he loved again. He had it all back, yet life made it impossible for him to enjoy any of it.

Life had a bloody sick sense of humor.

Morwenna moaned in her sleep, disturbing Robert's restless doze. The soft murmur, so close to the sounds she made when he took her—their separation hadn't dulled that memory—had his cock standing to attention.

As she shifted, he clenched his hands at his sides and fought the urge to grab her.

She moved again, with another of those damned husky sighs. He closed his eyes in agony. He should have taken Caro's offer to sleep in the blue room.

But he'd hated the thought of being shut away from Morwenna, when at last he'd found her. And there had also been the childish need to stake his territory. By then, Garson had gone, but Robert couldn't help thumbing his nose at his rival.

See? She's sleeping with me tonight, you thieving scoundrel.

I'm the king of the castle.

He didn't feel like the king of the castle. He felt lonely and unloved and bereft, like a dog left to starve outside an inn full of carousing travelers. Bliss hovered so close, he could smell it. Yet it remained denied.

Actually he really could smell bliss. Morwenna had straightened out, and her wriggling released the humid scent of her skin. Floral soap with a salty hint of warm woman.

Although he knew it would extend his torture, he sucked in a lung full of Morwenna-tinged air. Through the filth and stink of the pirates' camp, he'd struggled to recall that particular perfume. But he'd never been able to summon every subtle note.

Now her scent filled his head, as familiar as if he'd slept beside her last night. And every night since the day they married.

He thought she'd settled, but she rolled over with another sigh. The sound held a troubled note. It was almost like she searched for something.

He knew that feeling well enough.

Just who was she dreaming of? Was she missing her lover Garson? If she spoke the bugger's name, Robert might just lay waste to this pretty chamber.

When she curled in his direction, still without touching him, the breath jammed in his lungs. Every time she moved, he tensed up taut as a sail in a high wind. He wanted her touch. God alone knew how much he wanted it. But if she got too close, he couldn't rely on his control.

Her head tossed on the pillow, and she gave a mew of displeasure.

Robert wanted to comfort her. He heard distress now, and however much he might question her faithfulness, he couldn't bear her suffering. From the first, he'd have cut off his arm to save her from pain.

Then she wriggled closer and pressed that soft, sweet, damnably female body against his side. A lusciously round breast cushioned his arm.

She sucked in a shuddering breath, then released a deep exhalation of what sounded like contentment. Her arm in its silky sleeve snaked across his chest, and she cuddled into him, laying her head on his shoulder.

His heart stopped, then slammed against his ribs. His head buzzed with her nearness, and the shameful tears he'd fought all night pricked at his eyes. Just so had she slept beside him during the few weeks when they'd been together. Just so had she rubbed her cheek against his skin in a wordless declaration of love.

How he loved her. How he wanted her.

And how the devil was he to keep his hands to himself, when all his dreams were wrapped up in one slender woman who clung to him as if they'd never been apart?

He squeezed his eyes shut and told himself that he'd lived almost five years without her. One more night made no difference.

But when he'd survived without her, she hadn't been snuggled up against him, soft as a kitten. She hadn't been so near that he merely had to twitch a finger to touch her.

The room turned suffocatingly hot. Although the fire had burned down to embers, and he'd nearly frozen when he'd stood outside, trying to gather the courage to come in.

He gulped for air, which seemed to be in remarkably short supply. It didn't make any noticeable difference to his troubles. His heart pounded as if it fought to break free of his chest. And his skin burned all along his side where she touched him. Thank God she lay still now, although the soft brush of her breath across his bare shoulder threatened to send him mad.

Since he'd been gone, he'd faced a thousand dangerous situations. He'd been in constant pain and fear for his life. He'd suffered torture and injury and fever.

Nothing compared to the agony of lying beside the wife he loved and restraining his impulse to take her.

Fate continued to have a laugh at his expense.

Just as he whispered a prayer of gratitude for her stillness, she started to wriggle again, nudging closer. This time, blast her, she used her hands.

At first, he thought the soft strokes across his chest were purposeless. He could almost resist, when he knew her actions verged on innocence.

Then that seeking hand drifted lower. His belly shrank away from her touch, but the heat seared him from head to toe.

Impossible to resist when her hand ventured further and curled around his cock. He'd imagined he couldn't get any harder, but the touch of Morwenna's fingers almost sent him shooting out of the bed.

She made a sleepy sound of satisfaction and tightened her grip until he saw stars.

When they'd first met, she'd been sweetly virginal. But she'd soon become a lover whose passion had fueled his fantasies for the past five years. Hell, he wasn't sure he'd have survived his privations—and nor would his sanity have survived either—if he hadn't been able to escape into his head to relive their sultry nights.

Her touch was beguilingly clumsy. But before he could ponder what that might mean, she crushed her hot face into his bicep and kissed him.

The subtle movement of her lips on his skin beggared resistance. Her poignant tenderness bypassed all his elaborately constructed defenses, and damn it if he didn't blink away a tear as he stared into the darkness. Since he'd left her, tenderness had been a cruel absence in his life. He was powerless against it.

With a groan, Robert rolled over and pulled Morwenna under him.

Morwenna knew she wasn't dreaming, although in a thousand fantasies since she'd lost him, Robert had seized her in his arms and risen above her in the darkness.

She was half-asleep, but she recognized that the living man was here with her. That this time at last she wouldn't wake empty and unfulfilled and crying. Sometimes she'd reached such a pitch of need that she'd touched herself to take the edge off her desperation.

Even as she'd shuddered in lonely pleasure, it had been a barren release.

She missed the marital act, but nowhere near as much as she missed her dead husband. The banal touch of her hand where she wanted to feel Robert, hard, vital, ardent, couldn't satisfy her heart's cravings.

But this time, Robert's presence was too solid, the details too physical for her to mistake this as anything but reality. His rich scent, heightened with arousal. The hot weight of his rod in her brazen hold. The rasp of the hairs on his bare legs against her skin as he settled between her thighs.

Her heart was racing. She caught one shallow breath, then another.

He hadn't spoken, and she, afraid to break the spell binding them, stayed silent, too.

As he positioned himself, she raised her knees on either side of his narrow hips and tilted upward. The dying fire gave enough light for her to catch the gleam of his black eyes. He was staring down into her face, but she couldn't begin to guess what he saw. Was he in the grip of a purely animal impulse? She wasn't sure he was aware of what he did.

Perhaps it was wrong to surrender like this, when they had so much still to resolve. Perhaps for her pride's sake, she should wait for him to court her again, so he felt she was worth winning.

But sorrow and pride made bad friends. She was overwhelmingly grateful that her husband was alive. If he wanted her, he could have her. However he chose.

Tender. Slow. Quick.

She'd expected swift and rough, but before accepting her unspoken invitation to thrust inside her body, he paused. She curled her arms around his back, holding tight, daring fate to steal him away again. At this moment, she didn't particularly care if he didn't love her. As long as he was here and not drowned.

She hadn't expected any consideration, was so desperate to feel him moving inside her, she didn't seek it. But he bent his head, and for the first time in five years, her husband kissed her.

It wasn't gentle. It wasn't sweet. Instead, it was a primitive claiming.

She gloried in every heated moment.

His tongue thrust forward, demanding entrance. Shock held her still, until he nipped at her lower lip and on a muffled gasp, she opened. Immediate passion rose. There was no grace in this famished meeting of mouths. Teeth, lips, tongues clashed like a war.

She gave a whimper of helpless pleasure and sucked

his tongue deep into her mouth. He tasted like heaven. She angled higher and dug her fingernails into his back.

Kissing her as if he starved, he shoved her night-dress out of the way and thrust his hand between her legs. She'd been wet before she even realized that he meant to take her. When his fingers found her dripping, he gave a growl of approval against her lips. He was breathing hard, and she felt each unsteady inhalation under her palms.

He stroked her deep, but didn't linger to bring her to climax. She didn't care. She was close to coming with his kisses, rough as they were.

He caught her hips with ruthless hands and pushed forward.

She gave a sharp, hard cry. Her unpracticed body contracted with shock. She hadn't had a man in her bed since Robert had gone away, and she was no longer used to hard masculine invasion.

Robert stopped, and she felt a ripple of sensation run through him. He was shaking. So was she.

Then she felt him tense under her hands until his back felt like warm granite. With a groan that made her ears vibrate, he slid forward until he was fully seated inside her. Her initial discomfort vied with a powerful wave of feminine satisfaction. Her trembling intensified, and every nerve sparked with incandescent sensation. Until the pain was gone, and all she felt was full and complete and possessed.

And however unjustified, loved.

She released a choked whimper and arched up in a silent plea for more.

Robert was lost to everything but the hot clasp of Morwenna's body. This was even better than he remembered, and by God, he'd done a lot of remembering.

He pulled back, delighting in the succulent slide, then plunged forward. More welcome. She tightened around him and gave another of those damnable little sighs that had caused the problem in the first place.

The craving for release was a storm inside him. Every muscle tightened to agony. He shifted again. To his shame, he couldn't hold on. It had been too long, and he wanted her too much.

Then just as the tide of fiery darkness overtook him, he felt her shudder with the ultimate response, and she cried out again.

Robert plunged into her and let an eon of bitterness and misery and loneliness flood out of him in a torrent of hot bliss. He filled her with every drop of his essence and collapsed upon her, exhausted, cleansed, finally understanding that he was home to stay.

When he buried his head in the curve of her shoulder, her skin was damp and fragrant against his face. Her arms twined around him, anchoring him at last in safe harbor. Her body quivered after what they'd just done.

He could stay like this forever, but he must be crushing her. Even scrawny from captivity, he was much heavier than she was.

He made himself pull free, inciting another sleepy murmur from Morwenna. Then, unable to let her go, he rolled onto his side and tucked her back against him. She was boneless and unresisting.

Weary satisfaction weighted his limbs. And the greatest satisfaction of all was that Robert now knew that during their long separation, his wife hadn't played him false.

CHAPTER FIVE

*R*obert stirred from the purest sleep he'd experienced since he'd left England on that last disastrous mission. Deep. Dreamless. Untroubled. He woke with a cock standing ready for his wife.

Automatically he reached across the bed, but his hand met emptiness. He opened heavy eyes to a shadowy room and a slender, dark-haired woman sitting beside the fire and regarding him out of unreadable blue eyes.

To his regret, she was dressed. She wore a pretty buttercup yellow gown with a high neck, and she'd tied that glorious tumble of black hair up in an elaborate arrangement of plaits. She looked beautiful, but too self-contained for his liking. He couldn't help recalling the wild, responsive creature in his arms last night.

"Good morning," she said steadily. She rose to pour a cup of coffee from a tray on a table.

"Good morning." He sat up and scratched his chest. "Is that for me?"

"Yes. You used to like it."

He leaned against the heaped pillows and accepted the cup. She remembered how he took his coffee, he was pleased to notice.

Given his choice, he'd have started the day with a vigorous swiving. But there was something to be said for a pretty girl waiting on him. For too long, life had been devoid of any touches of courtesy or comfort.

"Thank you."

"I've asked the servants to draw you a bath. I thought you might enjoy a good soak after coming off the ship."

He wanted to ask her if she'd come and wash his back, but last night's passion hadn't banished the constraint between them. He took a mouthful of coffee and set the cup on the nightstand. Then after a jaw-cracking yawn, he flung back the covers and placed his bare feet on the carpet.

His attention snapped to his wife who had made a strange squeak, and now stared fixedly at the pink curtains.

"Morwenna?"

"You're...you're naked," she said in a choked voice. Her head was turned away, but even in the dim light, he made out a blush on her cheek.

She should already know that, given what they'd done in the early morning hours. Dear God, had she imagined she was dreaming when he'd taken her? She'd been sleepy, but he could have sworn she'd been with him every glorious step of the way. Now he remembered her ill-concealed fear when he'd insisted on staying with her last night.

"I'm sorry. I only had the clothes I arrived in. Perhaps I should have tried to borrow a nightshirt from Silas." Although his brother always slept naked, too. He couldn't imagine that had changed. Robert was blushing himself. He'd felt like a beggar, turning up so shabby at his brother's house. "Or waited to come home until after I'd arranged more suitable attire."

She shook her head, although she still didn't look at him. "No. I'm...I'm glad you came straight to us. Even...even given what was happening here."

The engagement party, she meant. After last night, he was considerably less troubled by what he'd found on his arrival. She'd been palpably out of practice when it came to the marital act.

"I'll have to do something about clothes. I need to report to the Admiralty today, and it would be better if I don't turn up looking like a tinker. I suppose I'm still officially on active duty."

"But first you'll...you'll tell us what happened to you?"

"I promised, didn't I?" He wished to hell he could avoid sharing his experiences with his family so soon after coming home. He'd feel much more prepared to tell the story once he settled back in England. In about twenty years, perhaps. "What time is it?"

Morwenna cast him a nervous glance, then looked away again. He realized he still stood before her, dick waving in the wind. But it seemed too jejune to scuttle back to bed like a pimply juvenile caught naked by a housemaid.

"Just past eight. I doubt if Caro and Silas are up yet."

He'd lay a wager that they were—and waiting eagerly for him to tell them everything, damn it. "I'll bet Amy was banging on the door at dawn."

"She cares about you. We all do." Morwenna didn't smile, but her blush intensified, although he couldn't imagine why. With a helpless gesture, she turned and scurried toward the door. "I'll see you downstairs."

Morwenna sat with Silas, Caro, Amy and Pascal in the breakfast room, looking out on a wet garden and waiting for Robert. Silas had sent all the servants away, so the family had privacy for what promised to be a harrowing session.

"But did he say anything more last night?" Caro asked for the tenth time.

Morwenna pushed aside her barely touched eggs and shook her head. "Caro, he was exhausted. It wasn't the time or the place for a long conversation. I'm as much in the dark about where he's been as you are."

"And he wasn't angry that you were planning to marry Garson?" She'd asked that question only half a dozen times.

"He didn't tell me." Although she'd noticed this morning that the edge was missing from his manner. Perhaps the satisfaction he'd found in her arms last night inclined him toward forgiving her for turning to another man.

Then you acted the complete fool. What a silly goose you are, Morwenna. One would think you'd never seen a naked man before. And you knew he was naked last night when he turned to you.

"So what did he say?" Amy asked. She hadn't been as persistent in her questions as Caro, but it was close.

Pascal smiled at his tawny-haired wife, and Morwenna was struck again by his spectacular looks. Odd, though, how his beauty didn't move her, whereas Robert's much more rough-hewn handsomeness, even now when he was scarred and worn, always made her heart beat faster.

"She said he went to sleep, darling," Pascal said. "It's clear Morwenna doesn't know any more than we do. Badgering her won't change that."

"It seems odd," Amy said sulkily. "I'd have pestered him until he told me."

"Undoubtedly, brat," Silas said with a laugh. He reached out and took Caro's hand. "I imagine we're the talk of London this morning."

"I'm sorry for Garson," Caro said, then glanced

horrified at Morwenna. "Oh, I beg your pardon. You probably don't want to hear his name mentioned."

"I feel bad for him, too, although I can't be sorry that Robert's come back to us."

"And Robert slept through the night without telling you anything more? That's just unbelievable," Amy said, earning her a disgusted glance from her handsome husband.

"We went straight to sleep," Morwenna said, hoping the heat in her cheeks wasn't visible. Because of course they'd done more than sleep.

This morning when she'd got out of bed, a few twinges had reminded her that she'd done things last night she hadn't done in a long, long time. And there were chafed patches on her neck where his beard had burned her.

He used to shave twice a day to save branding her, but last night, she wasn't even sure he'd been properly awake when he created that glorious magic. He hadn't spoken a word, although she'd gathered from his incoherent sounds of pleasure that she hadn't disappointed him.

Or perhaps he just appreciated the availability of a warm female body, and any woman would have met his needs.

She didn't like that idea at all.

This morning, she wore a dress with a high pleated collar. When Morwenna had come downstairs, Caro had settled a thoughtful gaze upon her gown, but for once discretion had won out. Which was unexpected. Her sister-in-law wasn't renowned for her tact.

"Well, I think it's unnatural," Amy said.

Morwenna was saved from answering when the door opened to admit Robert. Her heart slammed to a stop, and the memories of last night ripped through her, made her blood surge with heat. Even bearing the mark of his travails, he was a man to make a woman look twice.

"Robert, old man, come in, come in. Let me get you something to eat." Silas was on his feet and clapping his brother on the shoulder.

Morwenna wondered if she alone saw the faint alarm in Robert's eyes as he surveyed the five people ranged around the table. She'd realized quickly that he was uncomfortable mingling with groups of people. Including his beloved family.

"Thank you for lending me something fit to wear," he said.

Silas smiled at Morwenna. "Thank your wife. She suggested I dig something out of the wardrobe for you and send along my valet Dobbs to help you tidy up."

"I feel almost presentable." Self-consciously he touched his newly cut hair.

"You're a proper gentleman again." Caro rose and moved forward to kiss him on the cheek, before she poured him some coffee from the silver pot.

He looked much more like the polished man Morwenna had married. He was cleanly shaven and dressed for Town. If the smart black coat hung too loose on his frame, it was a small flaw in his overall appearance.

"Thank you." He moved into the room to kiss Amy's cheek and shake hands with Pascal. Morwenna noticed his well-hidden reluctance and was glad she hadn't pushed him to explanations last night, desperate as she was to know what had happened to him.

"I gather congratulations are in order," Robert said.

"Yes, your sister made me the happiest of men six months ago." Pascal bestowed a fond glance on his wife.

Silas had filled a plate to overflowing with food from the sideboard and placed it on the table. Robert sat down next to Morwenna. She watched him so closely, she saw how he paled at the sight of all those glistening sausages and kidneys and rashers of bacon. Swiftly she rose and took the plate away before he was sick.

"You've all been very patient," Robert said, swallowing and picking up his cup of coffee with a gallantly concealed shudder. "I appreciate it."

Morwenna hid the loaded plate behind one of the silver serving dishes on the sideboard and brought him some fresh rolls. His glance expressed his gratitude. Silas noticed, but was sensitive enough not to comment on the rejection of his offering.

"Eat first," he said, earning a resentful look from Amy.

"No, it's best I talk." Robert straightened, and the flicker of a muscle in his cheek indicated the ordeal this would be for him.

"We can wait," Morwenna said, finding the courage to lay her hand over his clenched fist where it rested on the tablecloth. "It's been five years. Another day won't hurt us."

She wondered if he'd twitch her away. Under her touch, he was as tight as a drawn bowstring. But after a moment, he turned his hand over to lace his fingers through hers.

"No, you need to know." But instead of continuing, he fell silent and stared ahead at nothing.

"The last we heard, you'd been attacked by pirates off Brazil. You were shot and fell into the sea." The grim edge to Silas's voice reflected the pall that had fallen over the family when the news finally reached them. "Everyone we spoke to agreed that after that, there was no sighting of you. The lieutenant ordered a boat out to find you, once the pirates had been repelled, but nobody held out any hope. How the devil did you manage to come back alive from that?"

Robert shook his head, and his hooded gaze focused on his brother. "I remember the cannonball striking me in the shoulder and taking me over the side with some rigging. I must have hit my head. I came to, tangled in some ropes and colder than I'd ever been in my life. The ship was a mere speck on the horizon. I don't think they looked too hard or too long, by God. I was bleeding, but the worst was the freezing water. I managed to get myself up onto a plank, but I must say I thought my goose was cooked."

Morwenna had feared he might have trouble getting the whole story out. Last night, he'd had difficulty stringing together more than a few words. But as he went on, the account started to emerge more smoothly. In silent encouragement, she firmed her grip on his fingers. While the little she'd managed to choke down for breakfast congealed into a hard, cold mass in her stomach.

Sometimes a vivid imagination was a curse. She had no trouble recreating Robert's desperate straits at that moment. Wounded, alone, lost in an icy sea. She loathed hearing about his suffering.

"How did you get out of that?" Pascal asked.

"I drifted for a couple of days. Luckily they were rainy days, or else I'd have died of thirst. I washed up closer to dead than alive on a beach. Unfortunately it was the beach the pirates used as their lair."

"Oh, no," Amy said, watching him avidly.

He shrugged, but Morwenna could see that his attempt at nonchalance convinced nobody. "I think they had some vague idea of ransom. They threw me into a pit and left me there, but at least they gave me food enough to keep me alive."

"So you've been trapped in a pit all this time?" Morwenna asked, horrified. She pressed her free hand to her stomach to quell the urge to bring up her meager breakfast.

Robert gave a grunt of unamused laughter. She realized she still hadn't seen him smile. "No, after about six months, I managed to escape. I doubt I'd have made it otherwise. You've never seen such a fever-ridden spot in your life. Another winter, and it would have been all up for me, believe me."

"So it's taken you the rest of the time to get back to us?" Silas asked. "Couldn't you have sent word that you were alive?"

"Unfortunately when I stumbled into the nearest town, opinion was divided whether I was a pirate or a spy. They flung me into the local prison while they made up their minds."

"How long were you there?" Morwenna asked, nausea tasting sour on her tongue. How had he borne all of this?

His voice was flat, and she could see that he deliberately avoided the grimmer details of his incarceration. But she knew his travails had been horrific and unrelenting. She'd seen the scars on his beautiful body, and his emaciation, and the haunted look in his eyes. A haunted look absent when he awoke, but now back full force.

By heaven, if using her body gave him the briefest moment's peace, she'd happily lie down for him anywhere and anytime he asked.

He stared down at the untouched rolls on his plate.

"I managed to escape two months ago. I made it to the coast and wondered what the devil I could do. Luckily, the whaler that brought me back to London stopped for fresh water and took me on as extra crew for the voyage north. Even luckier, they were on their way home and not starting their hunt, or I wouldn't have been back for another year."

Morwenna sent him an appalled glance and met steady black eyes. He knew as well as she did how close they'd veered to disaster and a scandal that would taint the family name. Another year, and she'd have been married to Garson, perhaps the mother of his child. After all, it hadn't taken her long to conceive Robert's baby. Any children she and Garson had would be declared bastards, because with her first husband alive, her second marriage was invalid.

Morwenna realized with a shock that she hadn't yet told Robert about Kerenza. She braced to tell him, but Silas had started speaking. "It was one of the happiest days in my life when you walked in." His deep voice, so similar in timbre to Robert's, was thick with emotion. "None of us took losing you easily. Morwenna, most of all."

She released Robert's hand and prepared to hear him condemn her for accepting another man's proposal. But to her surprise, he reached across and clasped his brother's shoulder. It was the first unforced gesture of affection she'd seen him make since he'd returned.

Well, unless she counted last night's passion. But that had resulted more from desperate need than anything as simple as mere fondness.

"And you can't know how the thought of my family waiting for me kept me fighting to survive."

Silas made an attempt to move beyond the appalling details of Robert's imprisonment. "You won't know the children when you see them. Although of course they've heard all about their heroic Uncle Robert. And, my God, how Kerenza will preen now that her father's home at last."

CHAPTER SIX

Kerenza?

As he lurched to his feet, Robert's face must have shown his profound shock, because everyone around the table fell silent. Morwenna stood away from the table and retreated a couple of paces, regarding him with a distraught expression.

"I tried to tell you last night," she said, wringing her hands.

"Kerenza," he said slowly. A child? *His* child?

Silas, Caro, Amy, and Pascal glanced at each other and by unspoken consent also stood. "I'm afraid I've put my foot in it," Silas said.

Morwenna mustered a shaky smile for her brother-in-law. "It's not your fault."

Caro looked between Robert and Morwenna. "We'll leave you alone."

"Thank you," Robert said through stiff lips. He

waited until the others had gone, then stepped close to Morwenna without touching her. "Is this what I needed to know?"

While she didn't back away, she regarded him warily. She reminded him of the woman who last night had seemed afraid that he might do something violent. When Dobbs shaved him this morning, Robert had looked in the mirror and acknowledged that she had cause for her uncertainty. He'd arrived at Nash House looking like a complete villain. Little remained of the dashing captain she'd married. Instead she'd welcomed back a grim-visaged and ramshackle stranger with a saber slash marring his face.

"Are you very angry that I didn't tell you?" she asked in a small voice.

Was he?

He'd spent so long concentrating on basic survival, he'd lost the habit of examining his feelings. One didn't need the finer points of self-analysis to stay alive another day, when hope was so far gone, it was hardly a memory. One just needed the dogged will to endure.

Now he was back in London, and life wasn't nearly so simple.

"We had so little time together before I went away," he said thoughtfully. Since leaving her, he'd had plenty of opportunity to regret that. He'd found the woman for him, then they'd spent most of their first year of marriage apart. Now he'd made it home, that was going to change.

When a wry smile curved her lush lips, relief eased the tightness in his shoulders. At least she no longer looked ready to take to her heels. "It was enough."

"How old is she?"

"Four."

His daughter's age confirmed that she was his. Not that he had any doubts. Before last night he might have questioned the child's parentage. Morwenna had loved him, but five years was a long time to wait for a dead man.

"You feared you're not her father." A horrified light sparked in her eyes. Horror that turned to swift outrage. "When I said I had things to tell you, you thought I meant to confess to taking lovers."

As he opened his mouth, he knew it was a mistake to try to defend himself. "Well, I walked in on you getting engaged to that dunderhead Garson."

"He's not a dunderhead," she said hotly, drawing herself up to her full height.

"He is, if he wants to marry my wife," Robert said with equal heat.

"Your widow." She raised her head, haughty as a princess. Last night's skittish creature was no longer in evidence, thank God. "And you're the only man who's ever slept in my bed."

Why the devil were they fighting? Although he liked to see anger revive the spirited woman he'd wed. That vivid girl had never given him his way, just for the asking.

When he looked closely, he could see that he'd been wrong to think that their long parting had left her unmarked. She was still breathtakingly beautiful. But her loveliness now conveyed a depth and richness of character. In his bride, that had been just a promise of things to come. And the deep blue eyes that accused him of misjudging her were softer and wiser, and too familiar with grief and loss. She was no longer the carefree girl he'd married.

Of course, she wasn't. She was a mother.

By heaven, he was a selfish cur. He'd never before considered their separation from Morwenna's side. He'd needed every ounce of strength and determination to come back to her, and he'd been through hell in the process. But she must have been through her own hell while he was away. She'd spent all this time believing he was dead. What had that done to her?

"I know I'm the only man who's been in your bed," he said calmly, folding his arms and leveling an unwavering stare upon her.

She frowned. "How on earth can you know?"

"Because you made love to me as if you'd waited all this time, as if you'd missed me as I missed you. Surely you remember what we did together last night. It was spectacular."

"What nonsense is this?" She frowned again, this time, through a blush. "Of course I remember."

He dropped his hands to his sides. "You didn't say anything."

"Neither did you."

"I thought if I spoke, you might come to your senses about what we were doing and make me stop." More vile selfishness, damn it. But he'd needed her last night. Needed her like he needed air to breathe.

"Why on earth would I stop you? I...wanted you."

Heaven save him. Hearing her admit her desire in that husky, hesitant voice had him as hard as a blasted ship's mast. Hard and ready. And blessedly alone with her.

What he planned to do right now was audacious, but irresistible. "Do you still?" he asked slowly, his gaze unwavering.

Her cheeks turned a delightful rose pink. "It's morning."

He ventured a step closer, pleased to see she didn't retreat at his approach. "We've come together in the morning before."

She gave the door an uncertain glance. "In our own house when we weren't likely to be interrupted. This is Silas's house."

"And he's left us to sort out our differences." Robert crossed the room and locked the door with one determined twist of his hand. "Very considerate of him."

"Someone could come into the garden and look through the window," she said shakily, as he turned back to face her.

"Not bloody likely." Robert cast an unimpressed

glance out the window at the torrential rain. "It's like Noah's Flood out there this morning."

"They'll all know what we did," she muttered, avoiding his eyes.

He rounded the polished mahogany table until he stood mere inches from her. "They might guess."

"We can't, Robert. What about Kerenza?" Morwenna bit her lip, and the sight of white teeth sinking into that pink, cushiony flesh only made him hotter. "Don't you want to hear about your daughter?"

"Oh, yes. More than anything else. Almost anything else." He was desperate to bury himself deep inside his wife, but he hadn't completely surrendered to his primitive self. Last night, he hadn't asked her what she wanted before he went ahead and took her. "Are you really going to deny me, Morwenna?"

Her pale hands fluttered up to her throat, and she looked charmingly indecisive. Well, it would be charming, if he didn't feel like his balls were about to burst.

"No, I'm not going to deny you."

A potent mixture of desire and relief kicked him in the gut. He sucked in a great gust of air, and his heart thundered with building anticipation. With greedy hands, he caught her up against him and kissed her again. Somewhere at the back of his mind, he recognized that after all she'd been through, she deserved his tenderness, his care. But he was so ravenous for her, it was as if last night's fierce loving had never happened.

And she'd borne his child. This willowy body had

grown round with his baby. Thinking of that made him want her even more.

Their mouths met in wild union. He couldn't get enough of the taste of her. He sucked her tongue into his mouth, and she made a choked sound of approval. Then another moan when he curved his hands over her breasts, rolling the pointed nipples between his fingers through the frail barrier of her dress.

"By God, I need to kiss your breasts," he grated, hating how the high neck of her dress kept him from touching her skin. "Why the devil did you wear this damned stupid rag?"

She gave a cracked laugh. "Because this damned stupid rag hides what you did to me last time you touched me."

His hands tightened on the lush flesh. "I'll burn it."

"No, you most certainly won't," she said on a shocked laugh, even as he pushed her until her back collided with the wall between the two sets of French doors. If any blasted fool did decide to brave the rain and venture into the garden, he and Morwenna would remain out of sight.

A gasp of excitement escaped Morwenna as she hit the wall, then another longer gasp when he shoved up her frothy skirts, found the slit in her drawers and stroked between her legs. He met sleek heat, blatant evidence of female desire. He brushed his thumb across the center of her pleasure and basked in how she shivered with uncontrollable response. A rush of liquid warmth greeted his daring caresses, promised a fervent welcome when he thrust inside.

He kissed her again, all seeking and passion. His memory of making love to his bride was of sweetness and innocence awakening into fiery sensuality. But this woman met him as an equal, demanded her share in what sizzled between them.

When she tangled avid hands in his hair to bring his head down for more kisses, he was overcome with awed delight. It was his turn to shiver when she lowered those insistent hands to the fastenings of his trousers.

"Don't rip them," he muttered as she hauled on the buttons. "If you do, Silas will never let me hear the end of it."

She gave another choked huff of laughter, but he noticed she became more careful. Too careful by far.

"Damn it, you're driving me mad," he muttered, scraping his teeth along her neck until she trembled like a flower in the wind.

He'd wanted her last night. But this was more powerful. He'd never been as desperate for a woman, for anything. And her clumsy attempts to free him threatened to incinerate the last shreds of his control.

He brushed her hands aside and in a couple of rough movements, freed his cock. She gave another choked sound of appreciation, and her impatient fingers curled around him. The sensation of her hand pumping him made him shake and groan. He bumped his hips forward, as she raised one leg to curl it around his hips.

"That's my girl," he grunted and caught her buttocks, hoisting her up to position her ready for him. The rich scent of her need teased his nostrils and made his head spin.

The world had shrunk to black velvet heat. There was neither past nor future. Just this woman and her sumptuous passion.

"Oh, Robert..."

The sigh of surrender brought an end to restraint. On a long groan, he sank deep inside her.

"Yes," he hissed in reverence, as she clenched around him in immediate, astounding female climax. She was quaking and gasping, her breath hot against the side of his face as she struggled to inhale through shuddering ecstasy.

He held on—barely—as the ripples of her pleasure gradually subsided. Then he thrust once, twice, and gave himself up to her in a gush of endless love and need.

Even when it was over, the remnants of that mighty release left him shaking. Panting, he released his bruising grip on her hips and shuddered anew as her legs slipped to the ground, breaking the union of their bodies.

In gratitude too extreme for words, he buried his head in her shoulder where he'd wrenched her dress aside. The sultry scent of satisfied female flooded his senses and calmed the mad rush of his heart. She stroked his hair and made a soft sound of contentment.

"By God, you deserved better than that," he muttered.

He felt as much as heard her choked laugh. "I doubt I'd survive anything that was better than that."

Their titanic encounter had held no tenderness. It had been all hunger and demand. Twice he'd taken her like a man starving to death. And he couldn't swear that he'd be any more restrained in future. He wanted her too much. But this gentle massaging of his skull made him feel like melting into a puddle at her feet.

"Nonetheless I should have been kinder."

"Next time."

"Goddammit, I can't keep my hands off you."

"I know." Her smugness soothed the lingering turbulence in his soul.

Finally, he dredged the shameful confession out. "I hated telling them about what happened to me."

"I know you did. I'm sorry." She paused, and when she spoke next, humor warmed her tone. "But, my love, if you're going to feel an uncontrollable urge to swive your wife every time you describe what you've been through, I'm going to be awfully busy."

My love? Did she mean it? She hadn't yet declared her affection, and while what they'd just done proved that she wanted him, he needed more than her desire.

But he was achingly conscious that he'd been here less

than a day. They were still finding their way back to each other. It was too early to insist on vows and promises. Good Lord, last night, she'd been frightened of him.

"I want you so much. All the time. It's like a fever in my blood."

"I want you, too." Before he could respond to that, she went on. "Aren't you going to the Admiralty today?"

Blast, he'd managed to forget the world outside this room, and he didn't welcome the reminder. "Yes," he mumbled, pressing closer.

He wasn't yet ready to face his responsibilities. Home only made sense when he had his hands on Morwenna, so he was in no rush to return to the everyday. She felt like the one real thing in the midst of swirling chaos. God forgive him, in this place that should be familiar, but felt as strange as landing on the moon, even his family were like beings of another species.

"Would you like me to come with you? I could remain in the carriage." Still she stroked his hair. Every touch seemed to whisper, "Welcome home."

"I'll be hours, I suspect."

"I can wait." Then in a lower voice, "And I'll have something nice to look forward to on the way back. You'll be ready for me again, once you've had to explain yourself to the Admiralty."

He raised his head, curiosity getting the better of

his urge to sink into her and never come up for another breath. "You really don't mind?"

Wide dark blue eyes, shadowed with lingering passion, met his. "That you turn to me to ease your troubles? Of course I don't mind."

His lips twisted in self-derision. "Some women might feel that I'm not showing proper respect."

That somber gaze didn't shift from his face. "Don't you respect me, Robert?"

"I honor you with every second of my life," he said, his voice gruff with sincerity.

Astonishment lit her eyes, although surely she must already know that was true.

"Oh, my dear," she said in a broken rush and rose on her toes to kiss his lips. Odd that this kiss, totally devoid of passion, should lay waste to every defense in a way those extravagantly carnal kisses hadn't.

He cleared his throat to shift an inconvenient lump and made himself straighten, although his hands remained at her waist. He couldn't bear not to touch her.

"Now, my wife..." His voice sounded impressively steady, although he had to work like the devil to keep it that way. "It's time to tell me about Kerenza."

CHAPTER SEVEN

Morwenna straightened her yellow dress, although she suspected anyone who saw her must guess just what she'd been doing in the breakfast room. She took Robert's hand. Odd to think that last night, she'd been afraid to touch him. Now it seemed as natural as breathing. More natural, in fact, than it had when they'd been together after their marriage. Then she'd been so young and uncertain. Not uncertain of her love, but uncertain that she was a worthy wife to such a superior creature as Robert Nash, naval hero, London gentleman, and brother to a lord.

Now none of those worldly things mattered. What mattered was that she loved him, and he'd suffered so much, and her presence calmed the devils she saw in his eyes when he thought she wasn't watching.

"Come with me."

He followed with alacrity. "Are you taking me upstairs to have your wicked way with me?"

She regarded him in surprise. Not at the suggestion. Despite that shuddering encounter that left her weak-kneed and breathless, hunger still hummed about him. If she set out to seduce him, she knew he'd cooperate.

No, she was surprised because what he said almost sounded like the teasing, laughing man she'd married. He wasn't smiling, but the fraught air was absent. While not exactly at ease, he no longer seemed likely to shatter into a million pieces at the first provocation.

"You have to go to the Admiralty. And I need to tell you about Kerenza." She crossed to unlock the door, feeling the pull on well-used muscles with every step. "But when you have time, I'm at your disposal."

"Morwenna?" He sounded dazed. His steps slowed, and his hand tightened on hers.

She turned her head and cast him a searching look. "You're not the only one who has missed conjugal relations, Robert."

A spark lit his black eyes, and he pulled his hand free. There was a different quality in his curiosity as he studied her. "You've changed."

Her lips flattened. "Of course I have. I'm older. I've had a child. Not to mention that I spent an eternity alone and grieving for you."

He took her hand again. The ease of the gesture proved anew that he emerged from the frozen wastes where his soul had wandered for so long. "I wasn't sure at first, you know."

"That I'd grieved for you?"

"Yes."

She looked at him aghast. "Oh, Robert..."

He directed a burning stare at her. "Do you love Garson?"

"You know I don't."

"Then why did you agree to marry him?"

Morwenna blinked back stinging tears. She wasn't sure she was up to handling this inquisition so soon after succumbing to that stupendous climax. All her emotions ranged far too close to the surface, and she feared saying something to bring the bleakness back to Robert's eyes. She recalled the frightening blankness in his face he braced himself to tell the family what had happened to him in South America. She never wanted to see that expression again.

Sucking in a breath, she made herself answer. "Because it has been five wretched, empty years without you. Because Kerenza needs a father. Because while I might have felt like I died with you, I didn't, and I'm only twenty-six. Because Garson's a good man. Since you've been gone, I've lived in isolation, apart from when your family dragged me out into the open. But this season, when Sally Cowan suggested a second round of Dashing Widows, I decided it was time to be brave and rejoin the world. For Kerenza's sake, more than my own."

She braced for Robert to express his disappointment in her lack of steadfastness. But after a weighty
pause, he nodded. "I understand."

"Do you?"

"Yes." That spark, a distant echo of his old laughter,
flickered in his eyes. "Which doesn't mean I won't
knock Garson's block off, if he dares so much as a
blink in your direction."

She smiled. It might be childish, but she liked to
hear that Robert felt possessive about her. Because the
fact was that she felt possessive about him.

"Were there...were there women?" she asked, as they
stepped into a hall tactfully devoid of all other Nashes.

"No."

They started to climb the stairs. "I can accept if
there were."

He arched his eyebrows. "Can you?"

No. "If I must."

"You don't have to. Even if I was interested, and I
wasn't, I was kept in solitary confinement. And there
were no women on the whaler."

At least she needn't pretend to tolerate the thought
of him seeking comfort elsewhere. Although given
what he'd been through, he'd desperately needed a
woman's tender touch to lighten his suffering. "Then
no wonder you have such a powerful appetite."

They'd reached the landing. Before she could turn
toward her room, he swung her around and kissed her
so fiercely that he stole her breath.

The kiss was over in one blazing instant. A thrill rippled through her, and her heart pounded madly against her ribs. Dazzled, giddy, she stared up at him. His black eyes glittered dangerously, and the slash across his face stood out white against his skin.

She placed her hands on his chest to confirm that he really was with her. It still seemed like his return was a dream, even now when relentless hands gripped her hips and his tongue had just been inside her mouth.

"I have a powerful appetite, all right." His voice was almost savage. "A powerful appetite for you, Morwenna."

"Oh," she said, as a warm bubble of happiness rose to fill her chest and squash the possibility of further response. Instead, she took his hand and led him into the room where last night he had seemed such a stranger.

She hadn't yet solved all his mysteries, but she began to feel that he wasn't a stranger anymore. One thing was certain. The man she loved had come back to her.

Once they were safely inside, she shut the door and rose on her toes to press a kiss to his lips. This kiss was more thorough, and it left her head swimming and her knees weak. She curled her hand over his shoulder to keep her balance.

"I feel like I need to get to know you all over again," he said slowly.

Something in his tone pierced her rising excitement. "Are you sorry I'm not as you remember?"

His hand cupped the side of her face, and for the first time since he'd come back, tenderness rather than desire was paramount in his expression. "You are as I remember you—beautiful and fascinating. But you've changed, too. In so many intriguing ways. I look forward to discovering the differences."

That bubble of happiness expanded, threatened to break free and fill the entire world. Last night, it had been miracle enough that he was alive. But their growing closeness was a gift beyond her dearest dreams.

"Me, too."

He kissed her again, softly. "Tell me about Kerenza. I'm agog to hear of my daughter." He drew Morwenna to sit beside him on the brocade sofa near the blazing fire. "You didn't say you'd conceived."

She shook her head. "I didn't know until a couple of months after you'd gone. I wrote, but I knew you hadn't got the news because the letters weren't amongst the effects we received back from the ship."

Morwenna stopped to push back a wave of painful emotion. He might have returned to her, but the shadow of losing him lingered. Speaking of this swept her back to the black days when she'd wished herself dead and with Robert, despite the child growing in her womb.

"Those letters must be lost in the Admiralty somewhere."

"Perhaps you should ask when you're there." She started to rise, remembering that he had other commitments beyond those he owed to her. "Should we do this later, once you've made your report?"

"That can wait. This is more important." He pulled her down beside him and curled his arm around her shoulders. She leaned back, drawing strength from his touch. "I should tell you that I'm going to resign my captaincy."

She stiffened and sat up to stare at him in consternation. "The navy is your life."

"Not anymore. I've come home now, and I intend to stay. Can you bear the thought of a husband under your feet instead of away at sea?"

Bear it? She wanted it more than words could say. "Of course I can. And Kerenza will be in alt to have her papa living with us."

"I hope so." Then in a low, sad voice, "I've already missed so much."

Tears pricked her eyes. Bitter, acid tears like those she'd barely contained when listening in wordless horror to what he'd told the family. It was less than a full day since he'd come back, and she already felt like she'd lived through a lifetime of overwhelming emotion.

Now this opportunity to tell him about their child was painful and joyful in equal measure. She'd never imagined Robert would have a chance to know the mercurial, affectionate, scarily intelligent little being created from their love.

To hide how overcome she was, Morwenna rose and crossed to her dressing table. Last night, instinct had warned her not to drown him in emotion. He looked more human now, and less like a ghost. But she feared the slightest mishandling might put his fragile recovery at risk.

She lifted the leather case that sat open near her hairbrushes, so she saw its contents last thing at night and first thing in the morning. Another leather case stood on the facing side. Another leather case she looked at morning and night.

Only a day ago, she'd made herself put the second case away in a drawer as a gesture toward her new life. This morning, as hope and thankfulness flooded her heart, she'd replaced it in its familiar spot.

She hoped Robert didn't notice how she fumbled. Her eyes were so full of tears, it was difficult to see what she did. How she grieved to think of everything he'd missed while he'd been alone and wretched and in pain.

With a shaking hand, she held out the first case, open to reveal the two miniatures inside. "This is Kerenza."

CHAPTER EIGHT

"*A* picture of our daughter?" Robert's hands shook as badly as Morwenna's when he accepted the gold-tooled Morocco case that held two miniatures painted on ivory plaques.

"I have these with me always. This year, because I've been in London so much, they've been a great comfort. She's happy with her cousins at Woodley Park, and I love that they've become like brothers and sisters to her, but I can't help missing her. And of course, she's got adoring uncles and aunts."

"It's not the same as having a father."

"No." She paused. "But I did my best, Robert. Please believe me."

"I do." He caught her hand and squeezed it.

She sat beside Robert as he stared transfixed at the exquisite little paintings. As if he'd asked, she went on.

"She's six months old in the one on the left. The one on the right was done for her fourth birthday last June."

"So this is what she looks like now?"

Morwenna gave a wry laugh. "No, it's far too angelic, and she appears content to sit still. Whereas she was a nightmare for poor Mr. Danvers who painted her, and I only got her to cooperate when I told her I'd think about getting her a puppy."

"A clever little negotiator, then?" Robert managed to ask past the boulder of emotion blocking his throat. Almost fearfully he reached out to lay a finger on the delicate pink in the child's painted cheek. *His daughter...*

"Just clever all round. She's definitely a Nash."

"She is, at that," he said, staring down at this child he hadn't known existed until an hour ago.

"She...she looks like you," Morwenna said in a whisper.

"Yes, she does. And like Helena. The dark Nashes are always hellions."

Was it imagination to feel an immediate affinity with the striking child in the pictures? As a baby, she'd been all staring black eyes and thick ebony curls. His late mother had always carried a miniature of his sister Helena as a baby. The two children could have been the same person, down to the hint of temper and determination starting to peek from each infant face.

"She's got Helena's nose," he said softly.

"She has. I know Helena hates her nose, but I've

always thought it suited her much better than some sweet little button."

"I agree." He switched his attention to the more recent painting.

This child did look like a little angel, but he'd seen too much of the devil in the first picture to be convinced. The promise of character was fulfilled. He looked into eyes the mirror of his own and silently vowed that he would make his absence up to her. So far, his little girl had grown up without a father. But he swore he'd never let her down again.

"She knows she's loved, and she knows she has a hero for a father."

He shifted uncomfortably, unable to look away from the pictures. "That's doing it a bit brown, Morwenna."

"No, it's not. It's true. She's already talking about running away to sea and becoming a ship's captain like her darling papa." Pride and humor vied in Morwenna's voice.

"Is she, by Jove? What a little champion."

"I think you two will get along—she really is just like you. Well, you'll get along, apart from when you're butting heads. She's got your stubbornness, too."

"I don't know what you mean. I'm a perfect lamb."

She gave a choked laugh. "No, you're not. And I thank God from the bottom of my heart for that. A perfect lamb wouldn't have survived what you have. A perfect lamb wouldn't have lived to come back to me."

He tore his eyes from his daughter's face and saw that his wife's cheeks were shiny with tears. Gently he closed the leather folder and placed it on the carpet at his feet.

Last night, he'd have hesitated to touch her. Now it seemed natural to place his arm around her and draw her into the shelter of his body. Just as it seemed preordained that she should curl up against him, as if there was no place she'd rather be than at his side.

"I'm sorry, I'm so sorry," she sobbed into his chest. "I promised myself I wouldn't weep all over you and make you uncomfortable."

He leaned his chin on the silky hair at her crown and tightened his hold. "I'm not uncomfortable," he said, and was astonished to realize that it was true.

He'd been terrified that his family would engulf him in great waves of emotion that would wash away his barely maintained sense of who he was. When he'd recounted his story, he'd done his level best to avoid any dramatic details.

But while he hated to see Morwenna cry, her tears didn't threaten his grip on sanity.

"Curse these tears. If I could manage to keep from wailing like a banshee when you told us the appalling things you've faced, surely I can control myself when we're talking about our daughter." She finished with a hiccup.

"I'm sorry I upset you," he murmured.

"Don't you dare say that." She pulled away, glaring

at him out of drenched eyes. "I'm your wife. I should know what you've been through. If you can live it, I can hear about it."

What could he say? Her courage moved him to the depths of his being. He leaned in and kissed her in silent homage, then stood up. "Where are your hand-kerchiefs?"

She made a vague gesture toward the dressing table. He stepped across and found himself transfixed. "That's my picture."

She sniffed and blinked in surprise as she looked up at him. "Of course it is."

With unsteady hands, he picked up the miniature. His parents had commissioned it when he was promoted to lieutenant. He'd meant to order a painting to mark his marriage, a double portrait of the bride and groom. He'd never got around to it.

Back then, he and Morwenna had seemed to have limitless time. His ordeal had taught him many lessons, not least that life was short and unpre-dictable, and a man had to seize his chance when it arose.

"I was prettier then." The boy in the picture seemed unconnected to him, like someone he knew once, but hadn't seen in years. The artist was more skilled than the much put upon Mr. Danvers who had painted his daughter. The young naval officer looked brave and stalwart—and ridiculously naive as he gazed into the distant horizon planning gallant deeds.

"But nowhere near as interesting as you are now," Morwenna said in a thick voice.

He found her a handkerchief in a drawer and passed it across. "Do you mean that? I'm horridly battered, compared to the man you married."

She gave a short, husky laugh and sat up straighter as she wiped her eyes. "You're like a pebble polished to a shine in the rolling ocean."

He raised his eyebrows. "My bride has grown poetic in my absence."

She held her hand out for the miniature and studied it for a moment with an unreadable expression on her tearstained face. "Poor Garson didn't stand a chance."

Robert liked hearing that, although he knew it was unsportsmanlike to gloat. "You kept my picture in your bedroom, while you planned a new marriage?"

When she looked guilty, he was sorry he'd asked the question. "I finally made myself put the miniature in a drawer last night. And felt a horrible traitor that I did."

"And brought it out again this morning."

"Yes." She swallowed and sent him a somber look. "I'll never put it away again."

For a long moment, he stared back at her, a vow of love rising to his lips. But he beat it back. Despite the progress they'd made—and last night it would have been unthinkable that he'd ask about Garson without snarling—he was painfully aware that they'd only started to restore their bond.

So he returned to discussing his daughter. No great

effort. He burned with curiosity about her. "So where did the name Kerenza come from?"

"It must sound outlandish to you." Morwenna's lips twisted wryly. "It's an old Cornish name that I've always liked. We'd never discussed children, let alone what we were going to call them. And Silas and Caro already had a Roberta."

He gave a relieved exhalation. "Thank God for that. Roberta? No daughter of mine should be saddled with that burden. Did you call her anything else?"

"Yes, Charlotte for your mother." She studied him uncertainly as she set the picture on a side table. "I hope you don't mind."

"Mind? You couldn't have done better."

She looked charmingly shy. "Would you like to see Kerenza? I could write to have her brought to London. She could be here within the week."

He shook his head and only realized how Morwenna might misinterpret that response when he caught the dismay in her eyes. He spoke quickly. "I'd like to see her more than anything. But why don't we go to her? It would save time."

And he had a horrible suspicion that while he might gradually find his feet in the luxurious sanctuary of Silas's house, he mightn't be nearly as steady amidst the city's hustle and bustle. Especially as his return offered a feast for the gossipmongers.

Morwenna's expression brightened. "I'd love that." And repeating what he'd already decided, "I also think some quiet days in the country might be what you need. Although with all the children at Woodley Park, quiet might be at a premium."

A sudden longing to see his boyhood home gripped him. He'd spent so long convinced he'd never get back to his wife and family, he had a powerful need to revisit beloved places. If only to prove that he could.

He caught Morwenna's hand and raised it to his lips. "Let's go then."

"Yes." The sound was a sigh and her fingers tightened over his.

He loved the way she reacted to his touch. Her eyelids drooped, lending her a breathtakingly sensual air. His susceptible senses stirred, and he glanced toward the bed behind them.

Her lips quirked up. "You're insatiable."

"Do you mind?"

She shook her head. "We have a lot of time to make up for."

"We do. So?"

To his disappointment, she shook her head. "You need to go to the Admiralty, and I need to get ready to leave for the country." She paused. "Or we could pick up Kerenza and go on to Portsmouth."

"You've kept the house?" The neat little villa where they'd spent their brief time together.

"Of course. It held all my memories of you." She frowned. "What is it?"

He shook his head and struggled to speak past the

emotion clogging his lungs. "I'm not...I'm not used to making plans. For so long, I was never sure I'd see my next sunrise." He swallowed again, but still that damned rock jammed his throat. "It's...it's over-whelming to talk about flitting around the country as if I'm free."

"Oh, my dear." She touched his cheek with more of that tenderness as powerful as thunder. "You are free. I hope you'll soon understand that."

He shook his head. "I don't think I've come back to myself yet."

Although the fact that he felt safe enough to reveal his feelings to Morwenna hinted he'd traveled a long way along the road to recovery. Largely thanks to this woman he loved.

"But you've come back to me. That's enough for now." Her smile was tremulous, and her beauty struck him like a blow. What a lucky dog he was, to have such a wife.

His hold on her hand tightened. "You said you'd come to the Admiralty with me."

She shook her head. "I know I did. But I think you might do better with Silas. If you encounter difficulties, he's a man of influence. And those old men there won't pay a moment's heed to the hero's wife."

He sent her an admiring glance. The girl he'd married had been unworldly. He enjoyed this glimpse of a woman who knew how to get what she wanted.

But he had to clear something up. "I'm not a hero."

Dear God, he cringed to think of the days on end when his courage completely failed and hope disappeared under a mire of filth and pain and humiliation.

That tremulous smile didn't falter. "You'll always be a hero to me."

CHAPTER NINE

*R*obert approached the Admiralty with no expectation of a warm welcome. After all, apart from his scars, he had no proof of where he'd been and what had happened to him. But to his astonishment, none of the senior officers expressed any doubts about his story, which even in his own ears, sounded more and more unlikely with repeated tellings.

He received a hero's reception and was quickly ushered in to make his report to the Sea Lords. He spent hours recounting his experiences and imparting what intelligence he could share about the pirates infesting the South American coast. In the end, only Silas's influence managed to extricate him from the labyrinthine corridors of Somerset House and back out into the rainy afternoon.

His exhaustion upon returning to the closed

carriage demonstrated more than anything else how right Morwenna was to suggest a stay in the country. That, and his prickling resentment of the prying looks wherever he turned. He and Silas had had to leave Nash House through the back gate to avoid the crowds on the front steps, and people had pointed at Silas's carriage as they'd driven through London. Inside the Admiralty, he'd caught the clerks' barely concealed curiosity as he was ushered from office to office.

Clearly the news of how he'd turned up to spoil his wife's engagement party was all over Town. He couldn't blame people for their interest. Good God, if he wasn't its cause, he might even enjoy the scandal. But after his long imprisonment, all those avid, interested eyes made his skin crawl.

"Well, thank God that's done." Silas stretched his long legs into the well between the seats. "You should be officially out of the navy after New Year, and you're on leave until Christmas."

"Thanks to you." Silas had seen Robert's discomfort with reliving his ordeal, and had taken charge of most of the meetings. "They're even going to pay me for while I was away. You were masterly negotiating that."

"So they damn well should, after the sacrifices you've made for your country."

"I wasn't sure I'd get such a good hearing." As the coach lurched into motion, Robert placed his—well, Silas's—hat on the seat. "You have to admit it's an outlandish story. I could have been sitting on a tropical island with a dusky maiden on my knee, instead of locked up in a foul cell the size of a cupboard. How could they know otherwise?"

"Nobody who looks at you could question that you've been to hell and back." Silas smiled, his quirky features alight. "At least you kept your temper."

"It was a close-run thing."

"By heaven, I know. And despite the country being at peace, they weren't too eager to let you go."

Robert shrugged and glanced out the window. He struggled not to shrink from the noise and activity filling the streets. Had he ever felt at home in this teeming city? After such a restricted existence, London struck him as nothing but chaos and cacophony. "I doubt I'm fit for command."

"It's early days yet. Compared to the wild-eyed savage who invaded my house last night, you're almost civilized."

"Thank you," Robert said drily. He reached up to pull the blind over the window. He felt like every eye in the city focused on him.

"They've left the way open, if you change your mind and decide to pick up your career." Silas pulled down his blind, too, enclosing them in a private space.

Robert was shaking his head. "I've already lost too much time with Morwenna and Kerenza. I'm not signing up to do anything that takes me away from them for years on end."

"Well, I can't say I'm sorry." Silas's voice lowered

into seriousness. "We've missed you like the devil. And never mistake how Morwenna grieved for you. Don't be fooled by what you saw last night. She's been loyal to you since you left."

His wife had stayed faithful to him. The knowledge filled him with poignant gratitude. And wonder that she'd kept so steadfast, when all hope was gone.

"Do you think I don't know that? Morwenna and I will work everything out." He hoped to hell he wasn't being fatuously optimistic. He and his wife had made a good start, but he didn't fool himself that making a life together after so long apart would be easy—or quickly resolved.

"I hope so. You've found yourself a grand girl there, and losing you broke her heart. When she accepted Garson, it was very much as second best. Which is a pity for the poor devil, because he was in love with her."

Poor devil, indeed. Robert was surprised to feel a moment's pity for his rival. "I don't care. She's mine. She's always been mine."

"Delighted to hear it." Silas's hazel eyes held no hint of his usual humor. "If you want some advice from an old married man, make sure she knows you feel that way. It's been a damnably lonely wait for her, and I doubt she's ready to take anything for granted, least of all that you still love her."

"I do." He was surprised how easily the declaration emerged. Discussions with his brother had never ventured into such profoundly emotional territory before.

"I know." Silas's lips curled in a smug smile, visible through the gloom.

A thoughtful silence descended, underscored by the patter of rain on the carriage roof. Last night, this hiatus would have been uncomfortable. Brimming with the powerful responses that his return had stirred up. Powerful responses Robert hadn't felt able to deal with, not if he wished to preserve an ounce of pride.

Silas was right. He'd come a long way in a short time. God bless Morwenna. What little peace he'd found since returning, he owed to her.

A desperate longing, so imperative he could taste it, overtook him. He loved his brother. He always had. And he looked forward to getting to know him all over again. But right now, he ached to see his wife.

Robert had joked about taking her in the carriage as they rolled away from the Admiralty. It didn't seem such a joke anymore. When everything overwhelmed him, only the hot, wet grip of her body set the world turning in the right direction. He was likely to become a rapacious satyr before he was done.

The prospect of getting her to himself, away from the hurly-burly, was the promise of paradise. And he'd finally meet his daughter.

His daughter!

It was too much to comprehend, when he'd spent so long hardly daring to believe he'd see his next sunrise. An embarrassment of riches to a man who had once thought a crust of bread the height of luxury.

"With your permission, Morwenna and I plan to go up to Woodley Park."

"To see Kerenza?"

"Yes."

Silas smiled. "She's just like you. Without her, I don't know how we'd have survived losing you."

"So you don't mind?"

"If you go to Woodley? Hell, no. It's your home as much as mine."

Not true. But nice of his brother to say so, nonetheless. "Thank you."

"Getting away from London will do you good."

"I feel I'm deserting you."

Silas sighed and leaned back in his seat. "Being with a loving family asks too much of you right now. I understand—at least as much as someone who hasn't suffered as you have can understand. I saw your face when you came in last night. That crowd nearly undid you."

Robert's lips twisted in self-derision. "I'm better than I was, thanks to Morwenna. Give me a year or so, and I might even get back to normal."

"There's no rush," Silas said calmly. "You're home, and heaven has granted us the chance to see you again. We can sort everything else out as we need to. The main thing is to return you to health and happiness.

And if my sparkling company isn't the answer, I can bear it."

"Thanks, old man," Robert said. He realized with a surprise quite how careful his family had been with him since he'd returned, and he was devilish grateful.

"I'm damned proud of you, Rob." Deep feeling thickened Silas's voice. "I'm proud of your brilliant naval career, and that you had the good sense to marry that fine woman, and that you have such a cracker of a daughter. I'm proud that you managed to get through your imprisonment, mostly in one piece. And I'm bloody beside myself with pride that you didn't punch that officious Admiralty pen-pusher on the nose this afternoon."

Robert gave a grunt of grim amusement that hid how his brother's heartfelt declaration had moved him. There was no man he admired more than Silas. It was a shock to hear that Silas admired him in return.

"I came damned close."

"Believe me, I know. When that pompous idiot said you hadn't been working for the navy when you were in jail, and therefore shouldn't receive your back pay, you looked ready to box his ears."

"He nearly didn't make it out of his office." The brothers shared a glance of perfect understanding. "Vile worm he was."

Silas looked thoughtful. "You know, it's too early for you to make any decisions, but have you given consideration to your future? You and Morwenna are more than welcome to make your home at Woodley. The house is so big, we could set you up in private quarters in the east wing. And Kerenza would enjoy growing up with her cousins."

"Thank you, Silas," Robert said. "But I'd rather go out on my own. And I hope Kerenza will soon have plenty of brothers and sisters to keep her company."

"Hmm," his brother said, as if he understood exactly how mad Morwenna and Robert were for each other. Damn Silas, he probably did. There had never been anything slow about him. "That means you have plans?"

If only Silas knew how many lonely hours Robert had devoted to counting the mistakes he'd made and how he'd remedy them, if heaven ever offered him the chance. The miracle was that he'd lived to see a time when he might achieve what he wanted. "Of course."

"So if you're not coming to live at Woodley Park—and I think you should take my offer seriously—do you want to go back to the Portsmouth house? I know you and Morwenna are fond of it, but if you want a big family, it will rapidly become too small. Now you're leaving the navy, there's no need to live so close to port."

"I think..." Robert paused. Odd that even with his brother, he felt shy articulating his amorphous hopes for the rest of his life. "I think I'd like to buy a small estate somewhere and farm. I've got prize money and my legacy from Papa. I'd like to give Kerenza and any other children we have a life like the one you and I had growing up. Loving parents. Freedom to discover who they are. All on a smaller scale than Woodley Park, obviously."

"So you really do want to drop anchor?"

"And never leave home again. Yes. Although I imagine Morwenna might fancy coming up to London occasionally, having had a taste of excitement this season."

Silas was shaking his head. "You know, I wouldn't bet on it. We had to drag her here kicking and screaming, and while she's borne it all with a good grace, she'd jump at the chance to become a farmer's wife."

"I hope so. Although if she wants to come to London, I'll damn well see she comes to London."

"You seem to have sorted out your priorities."

His lips twisted. "It's an ill wind that blows no good, brother. Imprisonment gives a man plenty of thinking time."

"I'm glad. I know you love Morwenna, but I couldn't help feeling you loved the navy more."

Robert bristled and glared at his brother through the shadows. "That's a damn rotten thing to say."

"No need to fly up into the boughs, old man." Silas paused. "And for what it's worth, I don't feel that's true since you came back."

Robert sucked in a sharp breath. Silas's accusation wasn't true, had never been true. But if he must, he might admit that he could see why his brother had reached that conclusion. "I'd die for my wife."

Silas's smile was wry with understanding. "I think she'd much rather you lived for her." He made a conciliatory gesture. "And I might have an idea about that."

"Oh?"

"The Devon estate I inherited from Uncle Frederick needs a manager..."

Robert's hand sliced the air. "Silas, I appreciate what you're doing, but I don't need your charity."

Silas's short laugh was dismissive. "Don't be so bloody stiff-necked, and hear me out. I haven't been to Belleville in years, but I remember it as a very pleasant situation with a sea view. Just perfect for all those children you've set your heart on."

"Silas..."

His brother ignored him and plowed on. "The estate has rather slipped off my list of concerns in recent years, and when the tenants left a month ago, the report I got back from my agent is that it's fallen into sad disrepair. The bones of the place are good, but the fabric needs some work. A nice little manor house, big enough for a growing family. Good land, if gone to the dogs. Half a dozen tenant farmers who are badgering me to address the problems the last people left behind."

"So why don't you?"

"I am. I'm asking you to devote some of that famous naval efficiency to turning the place around. You'd be doing me a favor."

"I'm not sure..." Although despite the way Silas's offer made his pride prickle, he was powerfully tempted. The prospect of getting his hands on a neglected estate and turning it into a home made his mind whirl with possibilities.

"It would work for you, too, give you a chance to see if you like the rural life. I know you've got a lot of romantic notions of life on the land, the way landlubbers have romantic notions about the sea. But you've been in the navy since you were eleven. Try it, see if you can straighten out the estate for me. Then if you like the place and the family is happy there, I'll sell it to you. The land's not entailed, so it's mine to dispose of as I wish."

"That's very generous of you."

"Not at all. By all reports, you've got your work cut out. But I think a challenge will keep you interested while you're finding your feet back on land."

Robert frowned thoughtfully into the gloomy interior. Could this offer at least a temporary solution to what he did with himself, now he left the navy?

It was odd how few regrets he'd felt when he resigned his captaincy. Since he was a boy, the navy had been his mistress, the perfect place for him to exercise his odd assortment of skills. He'd never wanted any other career.

Like all the Nash offspring, he was clever. He'd shown a precocious gift for mathematics, so he'd taken to navigation with an ease that had astonished his tutors.

He'd also been a lad who hungered for action and adventure. And yes, perhaps less admirable, he could admit now that he'd had a yen to cover his name in glory.

Today, on the other side of his ordeal in South America, he acknowledged how trivial that desire for fame had been. Now he just wanted to retire into obscurity and build a life with the people he loved.

The irony was that, as the admiral who had interviewed him pointed out, once the details of his escape got out—as they invariably would—he'd be famous all over again.

CHAPTER TEN

*M*orwenna went downstairs to find Caro and tell her that she and Robert planned to leave for Leicestershire. She found her sister-in-law in the library, writing a letter. To her four children back at Woodley Park, Morwenna guessed.

Caro was a marvelous mother, and Morwenna tried to follow her example when it came to Kerenza. So far, it seemed to be working, although at times she despaired of her ability to provide what her high-spirited, fatherless daughter needed.

Fatherless no more, thank God.

At Morwenna's appearance, Caro surged to her feet and rushed over to give her a hug. "Morwenna, how are you managing?"

To her chagrin, that sympathetic question was all it took to demolish her hard-won control, and she burst into tears. "Oh, Caro..." she said thickly and hugged her dear friend back.

"Shh, shh, sweetheart," Caro murmured, rubbing her back.

"I shouldn't be blubbing," Morwenna choked out into Caro's welcoming shoulder. "I should be happy."

"Of course you're happy," Caro said unsteadily, and Morwenna realized her friend was crying, too. "We all are."

She let Caro draw her across to a leather sofa in front of the fire. Outside the rain tumbled down, and the light inside was soft and gray. The library felt like a cozy sanctuary from the real world.

"I am happy. But..."

Caro pulled a handkerchief from her pocket and passed it to Morwenna, even as she wiped her damp eyes with her fingers. "But it's all been too much to take in. And you've been so desperate to keep up a brave front for Robert."

Morwenna sent Caro a thankful glance out of eyes glazed with tears. "He's so afraid of losing his control..." Except for those moments when he'd moved inside her body. Then he hadn't been controlled at all. And she'd loved it. "It's hard not to turn into a complete watering pot. He's been through so much and...and..."

"And it shows, although he works like the dickens to hide it. It nearly killed him, telling us as much about his captivity as he did. And it's clear there was so much more, and so much worse. His courage breaks the heart."

Morwenna sniffed and gave her friend a shaky smile. "When he was talking to all of us, I just wanted to put my arms around him and tell him that he's safe now."

Perhaps in the future, Robert would lay down his defenses long enough to accept comfort separate from desire. But not yet.

As if Caro read her thoughts, she said, "And you're so afraid that he might break, because all that's holding him together is pride and that great, brave heart."

"The heart that kept him alive through his suffering. I really thought I wouldn't be able to control myself when he told us that horrible, horrible story."

Caro's smile was misty. "I was close to bawling like a lost calf. Believe me. And Lord, I thought Silas was going to blow it all by losing his grip."

"But he held on. He's been brave, too."

"The Nash men are remarkable. We're lucky to have them."

When Caro stopped talking to direct a searching regard at her, Morwenna realized her expression must have betrayed her.

"Morwenna, you do have him. Surely you know that. The only time he looks halfway close to his old self is when he's with you."

Nervous hands tore at the flimsy handkerchief. "Oh, I know he loved me."

She realized she'd used the betraying past tense when Caro frowned. "For heaven's sake, the man worships the ground you walk on."

"I don't...I don't think he knows what he feels anymore," she said in a hollow voice.

Caro made a disgusted sound. "Nonsense. He can't keep his hands off you."

She blushed, wondering if the family guessed what had happened in the breakfast room not so long ago. "But that doesn't mean he still loves me. He's been locked up for a long time. He has a lot to make up for."

Caro surveyed her with disapproval. "Morwenna, do you remember his reaction to seeing you with Garson? We're lucky blood wasn't spilled."

"But that was just..."

"Male possessiveness? It looked like more than that to me."

"There's no guarantee love will survive such a separation. Especially as he's come back so changed. You remember what he used to be like. The man who made every party sparkle."

Caro regarded her thoughtfully. "Does that mean you're disappointed in the man he's become?"

Morwenna surged to her feet in denial. "No, never. My love isn't the easy type of love that ever changes, however changed the man I love."

Caro looked pleased and leaned back against the deep brown leather. "Then why don't you credit Robert with the same steadfastness? He's changed, but so have you. It doesn't mean you love each other less. Time and experience change love for everyone. If you're lucky, they make it stronger."

"That's how it worked for you and Silas." Morwenna went back to torturing her damp handkerchief. "But who says it will work that way for Robert and me?"

"Who says it won't?" Impatience sparked in Caro's blue eyes. "Is he the man you want?"

"More than ever." She voiced thoughts she'd hardly admitted to herself. "He seems deeper and more true to himself now."

Caro's expression softened, and she blinked away another tear. "And so do you. You've both paid such a heavy price over the last years. Don't let all that suffering go to waste. If any two people deserve happiness, it's you and Robert."

Caro's words rang in Morwenna's ears as Silas's luxurious traveling coach bowled north toward Leicestershire. For several hours, her husband had watched her with a heavy-lidded gaze that hinted at carnal intentions. They hadn't spoken since he'd told her about his meetings at the Admiralty. Long conversations still tested his stamina.

"We could have waited until the morning and gone then." She gripped the strap for balance against the lurching vehicle. Robert had told the coachman not to spare the horses.

"Leaving today gets us to Kerenza all the sooner."

She smiled. "I'm glad you want to see her."

His marked black brows contracted. "Of course I want to see her."

"I don't even know if you like children. There's so much we never had a chance to discover about each other."

He still watched her like a fox watched a rabbit hole. She shifted uncomfortably. That steady gaze disturbed her, made her blood thick with awareness.

"It will make life interesting."

She felt a mixture of relief and chagrin when he looked away toward the window. It was wet outside, but the rain gradually eased.

"So do you?" she asked, breaking the silence that fell.

He turned back to her. "What?"

"Like children."

He shrugged. "Before I was captured, I was a young man pursuing a naval career. I was interested in my ship and my wife. Not much else. The next generation didn't occupy my thoughts to any great extent. I saw a bit of my nieces and nephews when I had shore leave, and I liked them well enough, in the way a fellow with his way to make likes other people's children. Since then I've spent my time struggling to preserve my sanity. I'm still a novice with children, but I'll wager last year's pay that when I get the chance, I'll like my own."

"I hope so," she said doubtfully, even as she noted how much more smoothly he spoke now than when he'd first arrived home.

With every mile they traveled out of London, he'd looked less on edge. And younger, with the deep lines between nose and mouth no longer so in evidence. Dear heaven, he was only twenty-nine. He should look like a man with his whole life ahead of him.

He reached across and touched her cheek. The contact, meant as comfort, sizzled through her like a blast of summer lightning. How she wished she had the courage to ask him to ease this endless wanting. They'd changed horses twenty minutes ago, so they had guaranteed privacy for miles ahead.

"When did my wife become a worrier?"

She didn't smile at the gentle gibe. "You know when."

He looked stricken and lowered his hand. "That was an insensitive question, wasn't it?"

"No," she said. "You're still feeling your way back to the world. And...and to me. I'm feeling my way back to you, too. We need to be kind to each other while we find out where we stand."

His mouth twisted. With poignant curiosity, she wondered if he'd ever smile at her properly. From their first meeting, she'd loved his smile. Robert had smiled with his whole face. Even on the stormiest day, his smile always made her feel like the sun shone.

"Being kind to each other is a good rule in any case." He paused. "I can't keep from thinking about you left alone to raise our child. A widow too young."

"Not a widow, thank goodness," she said, glad they were talking about this, despite her disturbingly wanton inclinations. They had so much to make up for, and however intoxicating his touch, words alone could bridge the gulf between them.

She hoped one day—pray God, it came soon—he'd feel ready to share the details of his ordeal. Not because she wanted to hear. Her response to his terse retelling had been so devastating, she'd need all her strength to bear the full agonizing truth. But because she could only help him to heal when she knew the extent of his wounds.

His expression softened. "No, not a widow."

Another silence fell, on Morwenna's side brimming with gratitude too huge for mere words to express.

Robert reached forward to take her gloved hand. "Tell me about the last five years."

Morwenna sighed, even as his touch made her heart skip a beat. How to cover such a long interval? "Kerenza has been the center of it, although I made sure she spent a lot of time with her cousins and uncles and aunts. I was so sunk in grief, I wasn't always the best company for a lively toddler. Your family has been magnificent, especially Silas and Caro. They couldn't do enough, and they've made sure I wanted for nothing." She paused. "Except all I wanted was you alive and back in my arms. Even Silas couldn't arrange that."

Robert frowned. "You haven't been living on my brother's charity?"

"No, you left me more than adequately provided for. I'm talking about company and affection and support. I think for Caro and Silas, I was a link to you. They took me in for your sake."

"And for yours. It's clear they love you on your own account."

"I hope they do. Just as I love them." She smiled, as she remembered how good Robert's family had always been to her. "And they love Kerenza like one of their own. I can't tell you how thankful I am that she's part of a family when she's at Woodley Park."

"I owe Silas so damned much," he said, with a hint of grimness. "I should have stayed in London."

She shook her head. "They see what it's like for you. You find too much company...painful, don't you?"

He looked startled. "Is it so obvious?"

"To people who care about you, it is. We all know you need time and understanding. Silas and Caro are willing to wait for you to recover your spirits."

He shook his head in self-disgust. "In London, I could feel the pressure of them wanting me to fall back into their love. It sounds rude and ungracious, but..."

"But you're not ready yet. They know." She paused. "I know. And the house there was threatening to become a riot with all those people clamoring to see you."

"I felt under siege, even with Silas turning the visitors away."

While Morwenna and Caro had struggled to come to terms with Robert's miraculous survival, a constant stream of callers had arrived at the door. Some to offer genuine good wishes, most curious to see Robert returned from the dead, and a good number avid for gossip about the disastrous end to her engagement to Garson.

To her regret, Robert released her hand. "I felt like a wild animal on display in a menagerie."

"And it's too much."

"It is." His hands clenched on his thighs, and his expression tightened again. "I'll be an ordinary man again, Morwenna. I swear I will."

"Robert, don't be so hard on yourself. You only came home yesterday." She placed a soothing hand over one closed fist. Emotion turned her voice husky. "And for heaven's sake, you've never been an ordinary man. You've always been wonderfully exceptional."

He placed his other hand over hers, and she drew silent strength from his touch. She hated to see his pain and confusion. But at least he was here. She'd never imagined she'd touch him again, or hear his voice, or look into that beloved face, even sadly changed.

"Thank you." He turned his hand to lace his fingers through hers.

He'd done that in London, when she'd touched his hand in silent reassurance while he'd struggled to tell his story. The gesture had moved her then. It moved her now. A proclamation that he and Morwenna stood together against the world.

"Your family just want what's best for you."

"I know." His tone was wry. "They were very careful tiptoeing around me."

"And that made you feel worse."

His fingers tightened, squeezing her heart at the same time. But then, he'd held her heart in his hands from the moment she first saw him. "You understand."

"They've been very careful with me, too. Sometimes the weight of all that love..."

"Becomes unendurable. That's why you kept the Portsmouth house."

Of course he understood her need for somewhere she could escape and be herself. "It was purely yours and mine. Everything contained a memory of you. And lovely as Woodley Park is, it's a bit overwhelming for a country girl from Cornwall."

"And it's not your home."

"No." Her free hand made a dismissive gesture. "Oh, listen to me. I sound like the most ungrateful wretch in creation. Believe me, Caro and Silas couldn't have done more for me. And Helena and Vernon have been wonderful as well."

"But you still liked retreating to Portsmouth?"

Her smile was wry. "I did. Just as I liked having

Kerenza to myself. And I had a good friend in the town. That's where I met Sally, Lady Norwood. Without her company, life would have been even lonelier and sadder. Sally is the one who persuaded Amy and me to come up to London to play Dashing Widows this season."

"I look forward to meeting her."

Morwenna smiled when she thought of her lively, stylish friend. "Actually she's Lady Kinglake now. She was the first Dashing Widow to find love. She married Sir Charles Kinglake last August."

"And Amy is married, too. To the man she was madly in love with as a girl. How on earth did Pascal prize her away from her beloved cattle?"

Morwenna's smile widened as she recalled farm-minded Amy's topsy-turvy courtship. "I'll tell you."

As she told the story of Amy's romance, something in her noted that this was the most natural conversation she and Robert had managed since his return. Hard to remember that last night, the effort of putting two words together had been beyond him.

Encouraged by his interest, she moved to other family news. New children had arrived, and the older Nash children had grown. Silas had been elected president of the Royal Society. His sister Helena and her husband Vernon, Lord West were away in Russia sorting out a diplomatic tangle. Vernon had long ago retired from international intrigues to breed champion racehorses, but this latest mission resulted from a direct royal command.

Eventually she paused. She reached a point where so much talking tested her stamina, too.

Robert leaned back against the seat. "By God, they've been busy, haven't they?"

"There's more. But that's enough to go on with."

Sadness shadowed his black eyes. "What a lot I've missed."

Oh, no. Had she been wrong to say so much? She'd sensed his hunger to talk about something other than his captivity. But all this news just underlined his long absence.

"I'm sorry. Don't imagine your loss wasn't a gaping wound through everything we did."

He shook his head. "I know I wasn't forgotten. But I wasn't just talking about the last five years. I've been away from my family most of my life."

"You love the navy."

"Loved. When I was a boy, it seemed the path to adventure and renown. But it's a young man's game. There are other adventures."

"You served your country, saw the world, made the seas safer, and had a wonderful time," she said slowly. "Don't let your captivity destroy your pride in your achievements."

"Oh, it won't. But I'm devilish glad the navy accepted my resignation today."

"So they really are finished with you?" For herself, she'd be delighted if he never set foot on anything that floated for the rest of his life. She wanted him close by and safe. But she was wise enough to know that only he could decide whether his soul had had enough of voyaging.

Robert gave an unamused grunt and looked out the window at the countryside wearing red and gold for autumn. "If only. They've granted me two months' leave to recover, then I suspect I'll be up to my neck in reports and committees and interviews. I've come back with valuable intelligence, for all that I spent most of my exile sitting on my arse in a prison cell."

"Your information might help to defeat the pirates."

"My report will probably end up in a dusty file nobody looks at." This cynicism was new. The man she'd married had been unashamedly patriotic and idealistic.

"I don't care," she said emphatically. "You did your duty. And I'm proud of you."

He looked startled and sat up straighter. "By God, are you?"

"Of course. And your daughter is convinced her father is the greatest navy man since Nelson." She gave a shaky smile. "In fact, I don't think Nelson gets a look-in."

"She's biased." He looked touched and charmingly diffident. "So, my dear, are you."

"Perhaps," she admitted sheepishly, although she meant every word. "Do you mind?"

He sat back and folded his arms. "That my beautiful wife is inclined to admire me? Not in the slightest."

It was her turn to look startled. "I'm glad you still think I'm beautiful."

"You're the most beautiful woman I've ever seen."

"Well, I haven't had a lot of competition in recent years," she said drily, even as she basked in his compliment.

She wanted him to find her beautiful. She wanted him to have eyes for nobody else.

He shrugged. "It wouldn't matter. No other woman can hold a candle to you."

How silly to blush like an ingénue. "I think you might be biased, too."

He arched his eyebrows at her. "Not at all. This is a matter of fact."

And as they rolled into the large coaching inn and the ostlers darted forward to change the horses, Morwenna realized with a shock that her tragic, damaged, troubled husband had just teased her.

CHAPTER ELEVEN

*R*obert returned to the coach and sat with his back to the horses. He and Morwenna had snatched a quick meal in the inn's private parlor while a new team was harnessed, but neither had been inclined to linger.

"I should send ahead to reserve rooms at the next change," he said, stretching out his long legs in the space between the seats.

"We'll find somewhere when we're tired." Morwenna looked untroubled. In fact, instead of complaining about the inconvenience of their swift departure, she'd looked increasingly happy as they'd covered the miles toward Leicestershire.

She'd always been a champion girl, ready for adventure. He'd thought her the model of a naval wife. He suspected she'd be equally adept playing the gentleman farmer's lady, too.

He realized he hadn't yet told her about his discussion with Silas. "Silas has offered us the tenancy at Belleville."

Morwenna frowned in thought. "Is that his manor in Devon?"

"Yes. The last tenants have left it in a bit of a state, apparently."

"Won't country life strike you as very dull after what you've been through?"

"Not at all." He hid a shudder at the idea of facing more of what he'd just experienced. "It will give us a chance to have a real family life."

"With Kerenza?"

"Of course with Kerenza." And God willing, a brood of brothers and sisters. "A peaceful life in the country. Just what I need. Will you come with me?"

"Of course I will. I've...I've missed you so much, I can hardly bear to let you out of my sight. I think you're going to have to accept a wife who is inclined to cling."

"I'll like that." He reached forward to grab her hand. Her touch immediately calmed the currents of disquiet running through him. "You're the one thing in creation right now that isn't playing on my nerves. Surely you know that."

Her blue eyes studied him, as if she sought to discover all his secrets. "No, I didn't."

"Well, you should," he said shortly. "It's only when I'm alone with you that I feel I can breathe. Every other person in this whole damn world, even God forgive me, my family, makes me feel like I'm suffocating."

"Robert..."

"At least you don't expect me to be more than I am."

"I want you to do and be what you wish. In these last years, you've had enough freedom stolen from you."

"A wife beyond rubies," he murmured, as outside the coachman steered the horses out of the inn yard. The evening drew in, but the long twilight offered them a couple of hours of travel ahead.

"Well, at least a wife who likes the idea of a farming life."

"You won't miss London? You looked completely at home in society when I burst in last night."

He spoke without resentment. Morwenna was always meant to be his. Garson, sadly for him, was a mere distraction. Although Robert had always loved her, this oneness was new. He'd felt it when he was deep inside her body, but the bond persisted beyond passion.

Although passion certainly shored it up.

He was more than ready to shore it up again, although he couldn't regret the hours they'd spent talking. He'd almost felt like his former self, discussing things typical couples talked about, and not his extraordinary history of abuse and captivity. But as he caught a faint hint of Morwenna's scent, his cock rose insistently inside his trousers.

"I've enjoyed the time in Town, but it's not my real life. My real life is Kerenza." She paused and leveled that thoughtful gaze upon him again. "And you, if you'll let me make it so."

"I'd be delighted." He reached over and pulled down the blinds, plunging the carriage into gloom. He went on as though he hadn't just shut them into a private space ripe for pleasure. When his wife must know exactly what he planned. "So you'll think about Devon?"

"Is there anywhere else you'd like to go, anything else you'd like to do? Or is it too soon to ask?"

"I've had plenty of time to think about what I want. I'm looking forward to retiring somewhere Arcadian with my lovely wife and my angelic daughter."

As he'd hoped, his small attempt at humor elicited a laugh. In the shadows, now his vision adjusted, he caught the gleam of her eyes. She watched him steadily, the way he'd watched her when they left London. He'd wondered then how long he'd last before he took her into his lap and slid inside her. The idea made his dick twitch with approval.

He went on. "Silas has offered to turn over a wing of Woodley Park. We could stay in Portsmouth, although God knows what employment I'd find. The town must be crawling with captains on half pay, with the country at peace. Or as I'd originally planned, I could use my prize money to buy an estate. If Devon doesn't appeal to you, we can go somewhere else. But I had a fancy you might like going back to the West Country."

Robert stopped to draw breath, surprised he'd managed so many words. He'd got out of the habit of talking when he was in prison, where he'd go days without speaking to anyone.

"Let's see," she said slowly, clearly considering the options he laid before her. "I'm drawn to a country life. We could try Belleville. If we find the estate unsuitable, we can reconsider our choice. As Silas's tenants, we can move easily enough."

"That's what he said. And if we like it there, he said he'll sell Belleville to us."

"How kind he is."

"He is. Although he warned me the place is in a deuced mess."

"I'm happy to scrub and clean," Morwenna said with a hint of wryness. "I don't come from the same exalted ranks as you do. I'm not afraid of hard work."

"I hope it won't come to my wife doubling as the scullery maid. I might be the younger son, but I'm well able to provide for my family."

My family. How he liked saying that.

He caught the glint of her teeth as she smiled. "What a lot you've accomplished in the short time you've been back. I'm in awe."

So was he. Last night he'd lurched into that party like a monster into a feast. He'd looked like a beggar and felt like a ghost. Here he was a mere day later, dressed like a gentleman, on his way to see his daughter, and with the outline of a workable future beginning to appear before him.

A week ago, he wouldn't have believed it.

Even better, several hours of privacy beckoned. He had a beautiful woman within reach. A beautiful woman he was lucky enough to be married to. "There's one more thing I want to do before I've ticked everything off my list."

His wife's low chuckle made his skin prickle. "Your voice goes all low and velvety when you're thinking about the conjugal act."

His lips twisted. "Then it's velvety all the time, because I'm always thinking of getting you under me."

"It's...it's thrilling that you want me."

"Good," he said, as burgeoning need defeated his fragile ability to string more than a couple of words together.

"What would you like me to do? Lie down on the seat?"

Her cooperation shot a jolt of heat through him. He lowered his hand to undo his trousers. His cock sprang free, hard and demanding and ready for action. Over the creak of the carriage, Morwenna's faint squeak of excitement was audible.

"No, not this time. I want you to come here and kneel over me."

With a rustle of skirts, she scrambled from her seat and arranged herself across his knees. The coach's lurching made her breathtakingly clumsy. As they dipped into a rut, he caught her by the waist to save her toppling to the floor.

"Dear God in heaven," he gasped, as sleek feminine folds slid over the hot, tight head of his cock. "You're not wearing drawers, you naughty girl."

She shifted to find a more secure position, nudging her knees forward until they closed around his hips. The wriggling meant more wanton, tantalizing touches. He closed his eyes against the explosions going off in his head. He'd imagined he'd take the lead in this encounter. Now his wife's heart-stopping daring left him not quite so certain about who was in charge.

"Do you mind?" She leaned forward until her body curved against his. The bumpy ride turned the contact into delicious torture, nudging him against her, then away.

"Mind? You make me your slave."

She gave a husky laugh, and the warm puff of breath against his neck made him shake with need.

"You...mentioned...the carriage...when you...went to...the Admiralty." Balanced over him as she was, she had to speak in time with the bumping carriage. Bumps that tormented him with the rhythmic slide of her body.

"Yes, then Silas put a spoke in my wheel."

"I wish you'd put a spoke in my wheel," she muttered.

Before he could express his shock at her boldness, she shocked him again. She tugged his neck cloth free and scraped her teeth over his neck. He shuddered with response. His hands tightened on her waist, keeping her in place long enough for him to slip a small way inside her. She was lusciously hot and wet.

Delight held him still, or as still as the rattling vehicle allowed. "Mrs. Nash, you are a saucy wench. And I love it."

Almost as much as I love you.

His hold turned ruthless, and he brought her down over him. She muffled a cry against his throat and bit him. The sting intensified the wild sensations rocketing through him. The brazen clench of her muscles. The heat. The closeness.

The love?

She raised her head and leaned back. The shift in pressure threatened to blast him to rapturous oblivion. He stared blindly into shining eyes and lifted a shaking hand to catch the back of her head. He tangled his fingers in her silky mass of hair, bundled up for travel. Clumsy with need, mad with being inside her, he dragged her up until his lips met hers.

Their mouths slammed together in a succulent, open kiss of unabashed sensuality. She squirmed around him, taking him deeper. He felt he drowned in Morwenna. It was a marvelous sensation.

The fast-moving carriage shifted them up and down, and she tugged away from his lips, gasping. For a few dizzying moments, she moved against the rise and fall, then in one incandescent instant, she found the knack and started to ride him as smoothly as a rider on a cantering horse.

Heat surged through him, and the urge to lift his hips and fill her with his seed was nigh irresistible. But she was enjoying every moment of what they did, whimpering and sighing with rising pleasure. He couldn't bear to bring the encounter to a quick end.

Somehow he held back, although every satiny glide of her body threatened his resolve. He gulped in a great lungful of air, sharp with the scent of female desire.

She rose high over him, until only the tip of his cock remained inside her. He caught her waist again, afraid she'd fall. He glimpsed wild excitement in her eyes before she closed them and sank down. An expression of greedy bliss lit her lovely face as she took him.

His grip tightened when she raised her hands from his shoulders. "Hold onto me," she said roughly.

"Always," he gritted out, tensing every muscle against spending himself in her welcoming womb.

For so long, he'd battled the fear that he was likely to fragment into a thousand jagged shards. But inside Morwenna, he felt complete. Every time their bodies joined, he felt more like the man he'd once been.

She had such magic, his wife.

Morwenna shifted in time with the swaying coach, the dance of her body shooting explosions of light through his head. The movement was so beguiling, it took him a few seconds to notice that she was unbuttoning her green merino pelisse. He frowned as it fell open to reveal the darker green dress beneath. The bodice was demure, fastening high to the white lace collar. The contrast with her bare arse beneath her dress made him jerk his hips upward in a surge of desire.

She gave a broken laugh. "Don't move just yet."

"You're driving me utterly insane," he growled, flexing his fingers in the thick material of her skirts. He desperately wanted to touch her, but he feared she'd tumble into the well between the seats if he let her go.

"That was the plan," she said. "If I hold your shoulders, can you undo me?"

He wondered if she meant undo in the carnal sense, then his reeling senses focused on one detail that he should have noted before.

Unlike the gown she'd worn at breakfast, this dress fastened up the front with a row of carved wooden buttons.

"God in heaven..." he grated out.

"Is that yes?"

How the hell could she sound so lucid, when she squeezed his cock so sumptuously? He made an incoherent sound of agreement. Too incoherent.

She caught his shoulder with one hand and fiddled with her top button. "Because I can do it, if you'd rather."

"Damn it, Morwenna, you have no idea how I..."

Words failed him, as these days they were wont to do. She curled her hands over his shoulders and settled more securely on his lap, an action that nearly blew the top of his head off. The urge to rip the damned dress to shreds rose, but he bit it back.

For years, memories of her beautiful breasts had filled his dreams. So often he'd woken from restless sleep with his hands curled to shape those luscious curves. He'd loved her breasts from the first moment he saw them, a shameful fortnight before their wedding. When they'd been lawfully wed, he'd lavished endless attention on them.

Forcing back his need to spill into her, he began to unbutton the dress. It seemed sacrilege to fall on her like a starving man fell on a loaf of bread. But even so, he couldn't stop his hands shaking.

Control, man, control.

The collar parted to reveal a strip of pale white skin. He leaned in and placed a tender kiss where her pulse throbbed at the base of her neck.

Then Robert returned his attention to the buttons. Only half a dozen, but they felt like an infinite line.

Another free. More white skin.

Another.

He frowned. Perhaps female undergarments had radically changed since he'd been away. But shouldn't he see a shift and a corset by now? She'd certainly worn stays under that fetching blue gown last night, when she'd tortured him with the unlacing.

Torture? He hadn't known the meaning of the word. This was torture indeed. Morwenna heaving over him in a speeding carriage while he negotiated these pestilential buttons.

A line of creamy skin extended from her neck to the high waist. And no shred of linen between her and the air. Every drop of moisture evaporated from his mouth. Anticipation sizzled through him.

"Did you forget all your undergarments this morning?" he asked, loosening the last button.

"Oops," she said breathlessly.

The effort of resisting his climax already had his heart crashing against his ribs. Now it performed a somersault. "Let me make sure."

He spoke lightly, but he felt like he revealed a sacred mystery when he caught the edges of her bodice and slowly parted them. The shadowy valley widened under his gaze until curves rose on either side. His shaking intensified, and he licked his lips.

Quickly he raised his eyes to find her watching him with no hint of teasing. Her lips were full and glistening after their kisses. He kissed her briefly, then slid the dress aside to reveal her bare bosom.

"Morwenna..."

Again words failed him. In the gloom, her breasts were extraordinarily beautiful. White, fuller than he remembered. Hard, pink nipples like ripe raspberries.

Sighing in homage, he cupped her right breast and bent to draw that pert nipple between his lips. These lush breasts had suckled his child. The idea blazed through him like wildfire.

She started, and a gasp of pleasure escaped her. Her taste filled his head. Sweet woman. A hint of salt.

He tongued her nipple against his teeth, then gently bit down, glorying in how she shivered. She closed tighter around him. He scraped his teeth across the beaded peak, and this time, the ripples inside her tipped over into full climax.

She bit back a cry, and stretched into him, shuddering. He reveled in her pleasure, even as his balls tightened to the point of pain.

He gave her left nipple the same attention, as he rolled the other between thumb and forefinger. She whimpered, and he sucked harder until she lost herself again. She'd always had supremely sensitive nipples, but this ability to reach her peak when he kissed her breasts was new.

"Oh, Robert..." she sighed, voice husky with sensual satisfaction.

He couldn't hold back much longer. He squeezed her breasts, loving how they filled his hands. Then he reached down and caught her hips in a ruthless grip. The gentle friction of her body against his became a pleasure too tantalizing.

"Hold on," he grunted, tensing his loins.

She jerked in his arms, then remarkably he felt her

claim another climax. As her broken cry echoed around the carriage, he moved inside her until the world turned to fire. The surge started in his feet and flooded upward, through his aching balls. He filled her with every drop of his essence, while she trembled through the last of her rapture.

He snapped the bonds of earth and soared into some new world. Even after he was drained, his hips kept jerking. He couldn't bear this bliss to end.

Finally he collapsed against the seat and hauled her into his arms. He was still inside her, and they were both shaking. In the aftermath to those transcendent minutes, he felt her wriggle up to kiss him under the jaw.

"Welcome home, my darling," Morwenna whispered.

CHAPTER TWELVE

*L*ate the next afternoon, the carriage rolled into Woodley Park, Silas's beautiful estate in the Leicestershire countryside.

Morwenna glanced across at Robert. He'd been quiet for hours. Not that he was ever talkative these days. But since morning, her attempts at conversation had fallen completely flat.

After yesterday's extraordinary encounter in the carriage—recollecting that feverish coupling made her flush with pleasure—and using her body last night, he'd seemed more at ease. But as they got closer to Woodley Park, he returned to the taciturn stranger who had arrived off the whaler.

She supposed he brooded about everything he'd missed. How could she blame him? If she could, she'd bundle all those special moments up and give them to him. Kerenza's birth. Her first step. Her first word. Her first ride. Every birthday. A thousand sweet memories of their child discovering the world.

The tragedy was that those memories were lost to him forever.

Father and daughter, so alike, were strangers to each other.

That made Morwenna angry. Futile anger at targets beyond her reach. The navy. The pirates. Those idiots who locked Robert up as a spy, instead of sending him back to the wife who loved him.

Life. Fate. God's will.

As the carriage came to a stop in front of the columned portico, she glanced at Robert again. He looked stern and determined, as if he took on a deadly enemy instead of approached the daughter he'd never met. All day, his air had been grim. She'd known better than to suggest a repeat of yesterday's wildly sensual escapade.

Morwenna bit back a plea for him to adopt a friendlier manner. Looking like he did now, he'd terrify poor Kerenza.

A footman advanced to open the door. Robert stepped down and raised a hand to help Morwenna. When she curled her hand around his elbow, she bit back a dismayed exclamation. His arm was rigid with tension. He was as close to shattering as he'd been that first night.

Without speaking, Robert escorted her up the stone stairs to the massive double doors.

"Mrs. Nash..." Ballard, the butler, began. Then for the first time since she'd started coming here, Morwenna saw the real man overwhelm the perfect servant. He staggered back and went as white as new milk. "Mr. Robert..."

"Ballard, are you still here?" Robert moved forward to shake the man's hand. "I thought you must have long since retired."

At least he made some attempt to sound happy. To Morwenna's ears, it wasn't convincing, but the old man was in such a state, he probably wouldn't pick up the false note.

"Mr. Robert, in all my days..." The butler's eyes were bright with tears as he wrung Robert's hand. Morwenna saw the footmen behind him exchange puzzled glances. They must be new since Robert's day.

"It was a sorry, sorry occasion when we heard you'd been lost at sea. Mrs. Ballard cried her eyes out. It took me a year to believe it. I kept expecting you to turn up at the door, bright and cheeky like you always did after some piece of mischief on the estate."

"And so I have." Robert clapped the man on the back.

"Aye, aye, you have at that. Well, bless my soul. Will you come down to the kitchen and see Mrs. Ballard? When we got the dreadful news, she took on like it was one of our own gone missing."

"Of course I will. But first we're here to see Keren-za," Robert said gently.

Morwenna saw how this show of sentiment wore at him—he'd come a long way in two days, but his captivity laid a heavy burden on his soul. She couldn't help but be glad that they'd escaped London, where reunions were likely to come thick and fast.

She stepped up and placed her hand on Robert's arm. As expected, his frightening tension hadn't eased. "Ballard, where is Miss Kerenza?"

The butler released Robert at last, and she admired the way her husband hid his relief to save the old man's feelings. Ballard turned away and fished out a hand-kerchief to blow his nose, while the footmen struggled to stay expressionless. "I'll...I'll send for her, Mrs. Nash."

Morwenna shook her head. "It might be better if we go to her. Are the children having supper in the nursery?"

"Because the day is so fine, Miss Carroll let them play an extra hour in the garden."

Morwenna nodded. "In that case, we'll find her there. Could you please have my room made up and let Mrs. Ballard know that we'll be in for dinner?"

Under her instructions, Ballard straightened and became again the perfect butler, although a brightness in his eyes betrayed lingering emotion. "Very good, madam."

Morwenna took Robert's arm and led him through the hall and down a corridor to the morning room. He accompanied her with a docility that worried her. His eyes were glazed, and that telltale muscle pulsed in his scarred cheek.

"Do you want to stop and look around the house first?" she murmured.

This was where he'd grown up. Seeing it again, when he must so often have despaired of returning alive, surely tested him.

He shook his head. "No."

She firmed her grip on his arm. "We could leave seeing Kerenza until tomorrow, if you don't feel up to it."

"I'm up to it." The look he sent her was fierce, like a caged eagle. "This is just a house, however many memories it holds. I've been without my daughter for five years. I won't wait another day to see her."

"Very well." Morwenna was surprised that despite his obvious tension, he got so many words out. The night he arrived, he wouldn't have managed. "I'm sorry if you think I'm fussing."

His glance was sharp. "You make a very good mother hen."

She bit back a retort and opened the French doors onto the terrace. She'd been so worried about Robert and Kerenza that she hadn't paid any attention to the day. But Ballard was right. Yesterday's rain had moved on. It was a glorious autumn afternoon, and long rays of golden light turned the gardens to enchantment.

Silently, striving to communicate her love through touch, she brought Robert through the formal gardens to the pretty little pavilion overlooking the rose beds. At this time of year, they were well past their best, but a few brave blooms clung to the bushes.

As if waking from a dream, Robert looked around in surprise. "This isn't where the children usually play."

Morwenna gestured for him to sit. "No. But I think it's best if I fetch her, so you don't have an audience."

"You're concerned about her reaction?"

Actually she was worried about both her husband and her daughter, but she wasn't prepared to admit it. Long term, she hoped that Kerenza and Robert would build understanding and affection. After all, they were so heartbreakingly alike. But at this first meeting, with Kerenza caught unawares and probably overtired after a day with her cousins, and Robert strung so tight, he threatened to snap, she was worried sick.

"I think she's going to be overwhelmed." That was true. "So meeting you somewhere quiet is the best choice."

"You know her, after all."

She shouldn't read that as an accusation. They were both on edge. "Trust me to handle this, Robert. You've loomed large in her life, even in your absence. We all talked about you so much that you've become like someone out of a story."

He frowned in quick irritation. "You think she'll be disappointed?"

"Not at all." The smile she gave him was tender. He

was so brittle, and so desperate for this to go well. "But meeting your gods in the flesh can be a trial."

He opened and closed his hands at his sides. "I want her to like me."

"Of course she'll like you."

"And I want to do this...right."

With a shock and not a little self-disgust, Morwenna realized that what she'd read as anger was sheer, stark, staring terror. Her heart cramped, and she told herself she wouldn't cry. But the great lump of emotion blocking her throat made it likely that she would.

"Robert, of course you'll do it right. Even if things go badly today..." Pray God, they didn't. For his sake, not Kerenza's. Right now, the daughter was much more resilient than the father. "We've got time to fix it. We've got the rest of our lives. We don't have to resolve everything this minute."

Her reassurances didn't seem to soothe him. That muscle still danced wildly in his cheek, and he stood so straight and tall, it was as if he had a ruler for a backbone.

She had a sudden flash of insight. Just so must he have steeled himself to come into Silas's London house when it was packed for her engagement party. He had such courage. It humbled her.

"She mightn't like me."

"She loves you already."

"Purely because of family stories."

Her lips twisted, and again she told herself she wouldn't cry. "And you think the stories don't reveal the real you?"

"Not as I am now."

At last she saw shame as well as fear. *Oh, Robert...*

"She knows her father is a brave man who served his country to the point of sacrificing his life. She knows we all love you." At last, she spoke the words that she'd kept back, not sure he was ready to hear them. "She knows I love you. It's enough. It's more than enough."

She read the astonishment on his face and couldn't bear to wait for his response. Anyway, the moment belonged to Kerenza. "Stay here."

She turned and rushed away in search of her daughter.

CHAPTER THIRTEEN

When Morwenna returned, she was holding hands with a small girl in a grubby floral smock. Without making the conscious decision to stand, Robert found himself on his feet. His heart pounded with anticipation. Anticipation that included a good dollop of fear. As he'd said to Morwenna, his experience of children was limited. And this child was his daughter, so he desperately wanted her to like him.

Morwenna leveled that thoughtful blue stare upon him, and he straightened as he drank in her silent support. Morwenna who loved him. Who had always loved him.

If she loved him, he couldn't fail.

The little girl huddled close to her mother's green skirts. Huge black eyes, so like the eyes that he saw reflected in his mirror, focused on him.

He read shyness, but no fear. That pleased him. He didn't want his daughter frightened of anything, let alone meeting her father for the first time.

Her father...

Since he'd found out about Kerenza, he'd struggled to comprehend becoming a father. But now he saw his child, he finally started to understand. An ocean of reactions surged inside him. Pride. Curiosity. Awe.

And swift and astounding and immediate, love.

"Kerenza, I promised you a surprise," Morwenna said softly. "Do you know who this is?"

Kerenza surveyed him with searching intelligence, then the black eyes rounded. "I think it's my papa."

"It is." Emotion thickened Morwenna's voice.

"You said he had to go away forever." Kerenza still studied him the way Silas studied his botanical specimens. Or in fact, the way Robert pored over a chart to plot a ship's course.

He'd never realized how powerful it would be to see himself reflected in another being. His avid gaze ate up every detail of those quirky, vivid features. She was beautiful. She'd be beautiful to him forever.

His daughter!

"When I found out I was mistaken, it was a lovely surprise for me, too." Morwenna's eyes were bright with tears, although he saw how she fought to contain them for Kerenza's sake.

"Hello, Kerenza," he said, his voice husky. His hands

opened and closed at his sides as he fought the urge to grab her close.

That considering gaze remained on his face as if she gathered all her thoughts together before she reached her conclusion. He had no idea what most four-year-old girls were like, but he'd lay a large wager this one was unusually advanced.

"Hello, Papa," she said slowly. "You don't look like your picture."

His lips twisted as he recalled the romantic figure Lawrence had made of him. Even at twenty, he hadn't been that dashing.

"I've had some adventures since then. Would you like to hear about them?" He caught Morwenna's glance, then looked back at Kerenza.

She nodded. "Yes, please. Are you going to live with us now?"

He swallowed to ease the constriction in his throat. "Yes. Will you like that?"

She frowned as she pondered her answer, and for a moment looked so much like his sister Helena that his heart somersaulted. He hadn't expected her to seem so familiar so quickly, but she already felt like the blood of his blood, bone of his bone.

"Yes, I will. I always hoped you'd come home."

"So did I," Morwenna said fervently, wiping away a surreptitious tear that escaped her ferocious control. "Now go and give your papa a kiss like a good girl."

Pride swelled Robert's heart to bursting when

Kerenza left her mother's side without further urging and stepped forward. Of all the qualities he admired, courage was the greatest. And his girl was clearly brave to the bootstraps.

Careful not to betray quite how overcome he was, he held out his hand, but let Kerenza decide whether to take it.

When her small hand curled around his, his heart performed another of those dizzying cartwheels. She was a champion, his Kerenza, and he pledged himself to her service as long as he lived.

"Please bend down, Papa," she said, as imperious as a princess.

And why not? By God, he'd like to find a princess to match her.

"With pleasure." He went one better. He crouched until his face was level with hers. This close, he saw details he'd missed when she stood beside her mother.

The thick black lashes. The tumble of hair, thick and unruly, just like his. The slightly aquiline nose that would lend her features character when she grew into them. A few freckles scattered across her cheekbones.

For a long time, they stared at each other. He remained unmoving as that bright, black gaze roved across his face. As if she did her best to memorize every feature.

A dirty hand already showing promise of adult elegance rose to touch the scar on his face. "Who did that?"

"A pirate," he said, wondering if he should lie. He looked up at Morwenna to check for disapproval. He met eyes shining with what he now dared to call love.

"The pirates took you away from us."

"Yes."

"But you escaped from them."

"Indeed I did."

A pleased smile curved her lips. "I'm so glad you beat them."

"So am I, sweetheart." Emotion crammed his chest to the brim. "And now I'm home, I'll never go away again."

"That makes me happy," Kerenza said solemnly.

He had to swallow before he could speak. "So do I get my kiss?"

She nodded again, still with that serious air. He found her solemnity charming. Hell, he found every little bit of her completely perfect.

Slowly Robert tipped his head forward. There was a vibrant, expectant pause before, soft as the brush of a sparrow's feathers or a butterfly's wings, Kerenza glanced her lips across his scar.

The breath jammed in his lungs. The moment was so piercing, it hurt. He closed his eyes against the urge to weep.

The kiss was over in seconds, but it changed his world forever.

"Thank you, Kerenza," he said gruffly.

She smiled with a sunny openness that cast light into the closed, dark corners of his soul.

"Papa?" she asked, watching him steadily. She seemed as fascinated with him as he was with her.

"Yes, sweetheart?"

"Can I have a puppy?"

The sheer, astonishing ordinariness of the question struck him with the force of a swinging boom in a high sea. Then something strong and joyful and indestructible surged up from out of his belly, and he fell back on his haunches and started to laugh.

The sound took him completely by surprise. He couldn't remember the last time he'd laughed just from sheer happiness. A certain black humor had helped him survive his imprisonment, but he hadn't laughed like this in years.

Before he could stop himself, he caught Kerenza up and kissed her on the nose. For a moment, he held the light little body too tight. Then when she wriggled, he let her go.

She regarded him with disapproval, but didn't retreat. "Papa, you're very silly."

"Undoubtedly." He caught his breath and rubbed one unsteady hand over his face. Damn, that had felt good. "Can you put up with a silly papa?"

She frowned, considering the question. "Yes." Then she returned to the most important subject. "So does that mean I can have a puppy?"

"I don't see why not." He smiled and brushed his

hand over her untidy mop of hair. It was warm and silky under his touch. "What does your mother say?"

"She says we move around too much."

"Ah, but that was before I came home."

An expression of unfiltered elation brightened that intense face. "So I can?"

"Morwenna?"

"How on earth can I stand up to both of you?" Morwenna's blue eyes glowed misty like the Cornish sea at dawn. She met his searching glance, then looked down at Kerenza with a long-suffering expression. "All right, you little monster, you win. You can have a puppy."

"Oh, splendid." Kerenza performed a happy skip, then launched herself forward to hug him. As those childish arms encircled his neck and she pressed a sloppy kiss to his cheek, he thought his heart must break with love.

"Thank you, Papa. Now let's go. I'll show you my pony."

As the child took his hand, he tilted an eyebrow at Morwenna. "Coming?"

With a tremulous smile, she shook her head. "No, you go. I want to check on our room."

"Come on, Papa," Kerenza said with a princess's impatience.

Completely besotted, Robert went.

CHAPTER FOURTEEN

*M*orwenna waited upstairs in her bedroom. After witnessing Robert and Kerenza's meeting, she'd needed some time alone to smile and wish, and cry over his vulnerability and sweetness and courage.

She'd been so afraid of what might happen this afternoon, and it turned out she'd had no reason. Father and daughter had quickly established an understanding. He and Kerenza had marched off in perfect accord, after that moving meeting that had left Morwenna fighting the urge to bawl like a baby.

Kerenza had come to find her an hour or so ago, bubbling over with talk of her dashing papa. Although the promised puppy was an equally favored topic of conversation, Morwenna noted with amusement.

The puppy had been a goal for a couple of years

now, since Silas's spaniel bitch had given birth to a
litter during one of Kerenza's stays at Woodley Park. If
Robert's return meant a dog joining the family, Kerenza's affections would be eternally engaged.

It was only when Morwenna saw them together
that she understood quite how alike were these two
beings she loved more than life. She'd always found
comfort in saying Kerenza took after her father. But
watching the two of them negotiate a friendship, she'd
found it almost uncanny how their expressions
mirrored each other.

She'd ached to fling her arms around both of them
and smother them with love. But that encounter in the
pavilion hadn't been about her, but about them. Dear
heaven, she'd felt privileged to witness their blooming
closeness.

One of the things Morwenna had found most
touching about bringing Robert and Kerenza together
was how prosaic the occasion had proven. She'd
expected tears and drama and raging emotion. But
while she'd had no doubt of the depth of Robert's
response to seeing his daughter for the first time, the
introductions had passed off with an ease beyond her
most optimistic hopes.

So she'd consigned an overexcited Kerenza to the
custody of a disapproving Miss Carroll and promised
she'd bring Robert in to say goodnight to his daughter.
Before she left, Kerenza had bestowed a sticky and

enthusiastic cuddle on her. Fenella Townsend, Caro's close friend and one of the first Dashing Widows, had perfect children who didn't seem to know what mud was. Kerenza, on the other hand, loved the stuff, especially if it was mixed with muck from the stables. Her dress showed evidence of a fun visit to the horses.

Then had come the moment that had slashed a jagged rift across Morwenna's much-beleaguered heart.

"Is Papa really home to stay?" Kerenza whispered, her face jammed up against Morwenna's ear.

"Yes, he is, Kerenza. He said he's never going away again, and he means it."

The warm little arms tightened around her neck. "I'm glad. I love Papa."

"I know, pumpkin," Morwenna choked out, as her grip on her daughter firmed. "And he loves you, too."

"So he'll be here tomorrow?"

The fears of an orphan child couldn't be banished so quickly. But today had provided a good start.

In fact, an excellent start.

"Yes. And every day after that."

"The pirates won't come for him?"

"No, sweetheart. Your papa is more than a match for any number of pirates."

"I know that," she said comfortably and squirmed away. Kerenza was an affectionate child, but didn't like to cuddle for too long when she had other places to go.

Morwenna had watched her daughter race away to the nursery and no doubt many tales to share with her cousins. For so long, Morwenna had lived in a world of grief and absence. It was surprisingly difficult to adjust to a landscape bright with hope.

But it seemed hope must find its place in her life. Her daughter was happy. Her husband was clearly beside himself with delight at his lovely little daughter.

And Robert had smiled.

More, he'd laughed. Morwenna had wanted to cry from sheer relief, because in that instant, the two Roberts she loved—the man she'd married and the man who had returned to her—had united into one beloved whole.

Morwenna had assumed Robert would seek her out, once Kerenza came inside. Perhaps whisk her away for a breathtakingly carnal encounter. The restless rush of her blood told her that his attentions were overdue. He turned her into a complete wanton, and she didn't give a tinker's curse. She had years to make up for, and he was welcome to tup her from Truro to Inverness if it made him feel better.

It certainly made her feel better.

But she'd put her impatience aside—barely—when she thought again about the afternoon. After meeting his daughter for the first time, he was likely to need some privacy to come to terms with his reaction.

Now it was time to dress for dinner, and he still hadn't appeared. Was something wrong?

He'd handled Kerenza with admirable aplomb. And he'd seemed happy to have his daughter to himself afterward. But had Morwenna overestimated his strength? He'd been so keyed up when he arrived. For Kerenza's sake, he'd hidden his uncertainty. But that didn't mean he'd taken everything in his stride.

Disquiet mounting, she went downstairs and checked the gardens and the stables—although he'd always been the least horsey of the Nashes, and without Kerenza's company, she couldn't imagine he'd linger there.

No Robert.

She came in through the kitchens where a tearful Mrs. Ballard poured out her pleasure at Robert's return. Morwenna escaped at last, once she'd promised to bring Robert down to see her after dinner.

Which would be a fine arrangement, if only she could find him.

Evening turned into night, and she asked Mrs. Ballard to hold back dinner. Morwenna was becoming seriously worried, although common sense insisted her husband had just gone for a walk and mistaken the time.

Except she'd endured an eternity without him. It was too soon to trust a kind fate to leave him safely in her care.

Since he'd come back, she'd struggled not to weep and fawn and swoon over him. But by the time she climbed to the sprawling house's attics, she felt hysterics might be justified.

It was pitch black under the roof, and her candle seemed to make the shadows loom blacker. Ballard ran the house like an admiral ran a ship, but even so, up here there was dust and the debris from generations of Nash occupation.

Morwenna sneezed, and looked around out of watering eyes. She'd been in this part of the house a couple of times, hunting out costumes for amateur theatricals. There were chests packed with extravagant gowns from last century. While the huge skirts struck her as bizarre, she'd sighed over the exquisite silks.

It was unlikely she'd discover Robert lurking up here. She'd only ventured up those narrow stairs as a last resort, because she couldn't find him anywhere else.

The further she explored under the rafters, the darker it got. Clearly she was on a wild goose chase. Her husband was probably happily ensconced in Silas's library, drinking Silas's brandy and wondering where the devil his wife had got to.

"Well, you're clearly not here," she muttered in frustration to the absent Robert, when she bruised her shin on a wooden chest jutting out from the wall.

With a huff of irritation, she turned to leave. She was annoyed because she was frightened. Over the last two days, Robert had felt less and less like a stranger. But now with him out of her sight for so long, she couldn't help remembering the half-mad vagabond who had barged into her engagement party.

Who knew what that man might do?

Then, as she took another step, something made her pause. Perhaps a barely audible catch of breath. Or a feeling that she wasn't as alone as she'd thought.

Or perhaps that bone-deep awareness that lovers develop of each other's presence.

"Robert?"

Was she losing her mind? Because surely he'd say something if he heard her approach. And given her clattering progress through the jumble, people in Liverpool would have heard her.

Anyway, what in the name of heaven would he be doing up here, all alone in the dark?

She raised her candle, sure she was imagining his presence. And revealed her husband sitting on a tin chest under a descending corner of the roof.

She was about to ask him what the devil he was playing at, until the light fell on his face.

"Oh, my dear..." she said on an escaping breath, while all her fragile hopes shriveled to nothing. Despair crashed down on her, turning her heart to lead.

What a naïve fool she was to imagine that he was on the road to recovery. After all he'd been through, a couple of days couldn't possibly heal his wounds.

Especially a couple of days full of the shocks that these had contained. Her engagement. The spreading scandal. Negotiating with the Admiralty. News of a child. Meeting that child.

Even a man who hadn't verged on breaking point would reel under such a barrage.

He leveled glassy black eyes on her. She wasn't sure he saw her. His face was bone white, so the scar stood out like a raw brand. Between his elegant hands, he turned a toy wooden ship over and over.

She wondered at first if perhaps he was weeping for everything he'd suffered, everything he'd lost, everything he'd missed. But when she looked more closely, the fact that his eyes were dry made his desolation somehow worse.

Morwenna raised a shaking hand to touch him, then thought better of it. Tension hummed around him like a thousand angry bees.

"Should I go?" she asked unsteadily, fighting her impulse to fling her arms around him and draw his head against her breast, to comfort him the way she comforted Kerenza.

But Kerenza, for all her quirks and intelligence, was a child. Robert was an adult man. A hug, however loving, wouldn't solve his problems.

He blinked as if struggling to make sense of her question.

"I should go," she said in a thick voice. She turned away, although leaving him in the dark, alone and distressed, went against every instinct.

He shifted infinitesimally. If she hadn't been so

attuned to his slightest reaction, she wouldn't have noticed.

Still, it was clear that he wanted his own company, and she was an intruder into thoughts too bleak for sharing. She stepped back so the candle no longer shone such a cruel light on his stark expression.

"No," he said, almost inaudibly.

CHAPTER FIFTEEN

Morwenna paused and regarded Robert intently through the gloom. "No?"

That muscle in his cheek was back to its erratic flickering. His face was drawn and austere, with the skin stretched tight over the bones. He certainly didn't look like he wanted her to stay.

She sucked in a breath that tasted of defeat. "I'll see you downstairs."

"No." More loudly this time. He reached out to catch the filmy material of her skirt. "Wait."

She cast him a troubled glance, but didn't retreat. When he realized she wasn't going to move away, he dropped his hand.

She set the candle on another chest and dragged up a trunk to sit on, disturbing a cloud of dust. She didn't touch him, but remained within touching distance if he decided he needed physical contact. "Are you ill?"

His lips twisted downward. "Only in my mind."

She shook her head. "You're not mad."

He gave a snort of self-derision. "It might be easier if I was."

"Don't say that." After what he'd been through, some men would have lost their senses. But whatever else ailed him, his wits remained as dauntingly sharp as they'd ever been.

A thorny silence descended between them.

"What can I do?" she asked eventually.

With a shaking hand, he grabbed her wrist, the way he'd grabbed it that first night. He wasn't gentle, but she didn't mind. She could see he teetered on the edge of disintegration.

"Just...just stay with me."

"Of course."

For a further interval, they sat unspeaking. Slowly his awful tension receded. At last, she took a chance on him being ready to talk.

"Why the attics?"

When he didn't answer immediately, she wondered if she'd made a mistake. Then he started to speak slowly, as if unsure whether he'd muster the words. "I was asking Kerenza about her favorite toy. She wanted to know what had been mine."

Ah. "The ship."

In the shadows, she heard rather than saw him put the toy down on the bare wooden floorboards. "Yes."

She could imagine how memories of his childhood

had overwhelmed him when he'd found the ship. Memories of his childhood, and his forsaken dreams of a brilliant naval career. "I worried...I worried perhaps you had a problem with Kerenza."

"No. She's absolutely delightful." He slid his hand down and linked his fingers with hers. "Just like her mother."

He spoke more naturally, but she didn't fool herself that he was anywhere near ready to come downstairs. At least he no longer clung to her like a drowning man snatched at flotsam to save himself from sinking.

"That's odd." Gently she squeezed his hand. "In my opinion, she's just like you."

"In looks, perhaps, although I think she's most like Helena. But her brightness and her joy are yours, all yours."

Absurdly she found herself blushing. "Thank you."

"It's..."

She finished his sentence when she realized he couldn't. "It's all been overwhelming."

His fingers flexed against hers. "Yes," he admitted in a muffled voice. "The change in my circumstances has left me staggering. It's only weeks since I was locked up, awaiting execution."

Horror rippled through her. He hadn't mentioned that before. She was more certain than ever that he'd kept the worst of his ordeal to himself to protect people's feelings. "It's too soon for you to feel safe."

His free hand made a sweeping gesture. "Coming

home has been like entering a mythical kingdom. None of it feels real. None of it, except you. And now Kerenza." He made an impatient sound deep in his throat. "It's hard to explain."

"Try."

He paused, then went on in a low voice. "I've spent five years freezing cold or boiling hot. I've never been clean, or at ease, or dressed in anything but rags. I never had enough to eat, and I was always in pain from a beating."

His hand clenched on hers to the point of discomfort, and she bit her lip to stifle a protest. Sour bile rose in her throat as she thought about his captivity. Yet she didn't dare speak, in case he stopped. In the cold light of day, she'd never get him to confess so much.

"Then I come home to a loving family and every comfort. It feels insubstantial, like it could all be ripped away in a heartbeat. It feels…wrong."

She licked dry lips. "Give yourself time."

"I know. But I can't feel I deserve all the blessings that..." His voice cracked and faded.

Unable to stop herself, although she didn't know whether he wanted her comfort, Morwenna leaned forward to run her hand down his cheek. The tender caress said all the things words couldn't. His beard prickled under her touch.

"Of course you do." Her heart threatened to crack. She loved him so much. If only she could make him see himself the way she saw him. As someone strong and brave and resilient, despite all the damage the world had tried to do to him. "You deserve everything marvelous that heaven can grant. Don't you know that?"

"No. No, I don't think I do," he said in a dull tone. He went on before she could gather an argument. "It's like every nightmare has turned into a dream come true. I'm back with my loving family. I have a chance at a useful, happy life. I have a daughter who makes me so proud, I'm ready to burst."

Warm moisture soaked the fingertips that lay against his face, and she was desperately glad that she'd shifted the candle away. These tears would help to heal him, but he hadn't yet abandoned his pride, despite this aching vulnerability. He'd hate to break down in front of her like this.

He went on in a whisper. "I have a wife who says she loves me."

For a moment, the words hung in the air, as if written in fire on the shadows. He had heard and understood her. She hadn't been sure.

Where did this leave them? She noticed he wasn't rushing to tell her he loved her in return. She lifted her hand away from his face. "Do you doubt it?"

"I did. I don't anymore."

"I know how it looked with Garson..."

He made a sweeping gesture. "It's forgotten. I know how you grieved. I'll never forgive myself for causing you such pain."

She summoned a smile, although she doubted that he could see it. "Yes, I was wretched without you. But you've also given me so much joy."

"Kerenza."

"Kerenza, of course. But just you. I wondered if I'd mistaken how alive you make me feel. But I hadn't." She paused, and spoke the words that had been true from the moment she first saw him. "I love you, Robert. Forever."

His hand tightened on hers. "The need to come back to you was all that kept me alive."

That was something. That was a lot.

Childish to be disappointed that he didn't respond to her declaration with a declaration of his own. She knew—who better?—the demands the last days had placed on him. After all this turmoil, she couldn't blame him if he had no idea of what he felt about anything, let alone the wife he hardly knew anymore. "I'm glad."

"So am I."

A silence fell, less fraught than the last one, thank heaven. Because the atmosphere was easier, and because it was dark and he wouldn't read the desperation on her face, she spoke. "I hope one day you'll love me the way you once did."

She heard a sharp intake of breath, and he snatched his hand away from hers. "What the devil?"

She summoned all her courage. "I love you. I want you to love me."

"Who the hell says I don't?" he asked, sounding angry.

She stood on legs that felt like string and wished she hadn't broached this issue now. Hadn't she spent the last two days lecturing herself about not putting any pressure on him? Her sigh was desolate. "I'm sorry, Robert. It's not the time."

He stood, too, and caught her arm. "Why in Hades don't you think I love you?"

"You haven't said anything," she said flatly, although she made no attempt to pull away.

"Damn it, Morwenna, I've tupped you every chance I got."

"You've been alone a long time," she said stubbornly, knowing she should let this go.

"And you're convenient? That doesn't flatter either of us." He sucked in a furious breath. "You should be able to judge my feelings by my actions."

"Why?" she snapped.

"Because you love me."

"And did you know that before I told you?"

"I hoped."

"Well, so do I. And I've said I'm willing to wait."

He slumped back onto the chest, his anger abruptly evaporating. "The last time I told you I loved you, I was a whole man, instead of a half-mad ghost, returned from the dead."

She bit back a gasp of dismay. Dear heaven, she should have realized what was wrong. Hadn't she already read the shame that lay beneath his relief at being home?

"You're a whole man to me, Robert. You're...everything. And I don't care that you're exhausted and scarred and eaten up with your agonizing memories." She bit her lip, cursing her inability to express what she felt. "No, that's wrong. Of course I care. But the most important things of all—the only really essential things —are that you came back to me, that you're alive, and that we have a chance to be together."

"But I'm not the person you fell in love with."

"Nor am I. I've lived through years of sorrow, and I've raised your child, and I've had experiences you'll never be part of. Does that mean you can never love me?"

"Don't be absurd."

She struggled not to take too much encouragement from that. Her wish for a happy ending had already caught her out today. She straightened and stared at him through the darkness. "Then look at things from my point of view."

"I have. I don't see why the devil you'd want me."

"Because I love you." She paused and swallowed before she asked the one question that truly mattered. "Do you love me?"

When he didn't answer immediately, her heart contracted into a hard little kernel of misery. Then his breath escaped in a heavy sigh, and he stared at the floor. "I'm not worthy to love you."

That sounded promising, if she discounted his stupid, masculine pride. "Does that mean you don't love me?"

He gave a grunt of laughter, genuine laughter, however sardonic, and lifted his head to stare at her with wary eyes. "Of course it doesn't."

She'd gone too far to let him get away without saying the words. "So you do love me?"

His lips twisted in self-derision. "You never used to nag."

"Robert," she said in warning.

He spread his hands, and she saw those straight shoulders that bent under the weight of so much loss loosen as he finally surrendered. "Yes, damn you, Morwenna, I love you."

Thank God. She sucked in her first full breath since this conversation started. New hope cautiously fluttered to life. Surely this meant that everything was going to be all right. She hadn't been mistaken to trust that now Robert was back, they could solve every other problem. It might take time. But then with him here, fate granted them a lifetime.

"You could say it a bit more nicely." She tried to speak lightly, but the tightness of her throat defeated her.

He loomed up beside her, tall and powerful, and above all *hers*, and she shivered with animal awareness. She'd only shared this link with one man—and she'd believed him lost to her forever. The fact that he'd come back remained a miracle in her eyes. She'd never take their love for granted.

"I don't know whether I want to kiss you, or give you a good shaking," he said drily.

His nearness warmed her skin, although he hadn't yet touched her. "I think I know."

He gave a low growl of frustration. "But first you want me to spread my heart out before you."

"Yes, please."

With him standing in front of the candle, she couldn't see his expression. But when he cradled her face, his touch was tender. The sweetness seeped through her like new honey on fresh bread.

She waited for more reluctance, but his voice emerged serious and calm and certain. "Morwenna Nash, you're the only girl I've ever loved. I'll love you until the day I die. Without you, I'm nothing. Now I've come back to you, I swear I'll devote every minute of the rest of my life to making you happy."

Oh, dear. Be careful what you asked for. It was her turn to start crying.

"For..." She stopped to swallow the jagged rock blocking her throat. "For a man who had trouble stringing two words together, you can certainly rise to the occasion when you have to."

Robert leaned in and kissed her. She tasted the salt of her tears—and perhaps a few of his, too. The kiss was gentle, the way they'd kissed when courting all

those years ago. And it held a poignant touch of innocence that made her weep anew.

Robert drew away slowly, as if he, too, didn't want
the magic to diminish. "Now, my love and my wife, let's
leave this place of darkness, and go downstairs into the
light."

EPILOGUE

Richmond Park outside London, May 1837

"*H*ere are Sally and Charles," Amy said, waving to the newcomers from where she stood with Morwenna on a rise above the river.

As her friends' elegant carriage rolled onto the broad field beside the Thames, Morwenna looked up from the baby daughter sleeping in her arms. Now everyone she loved was here, it was a celebration indeed. "Oh, how lovely. I thought they might have stayed in Italy this spring."

"You know they hate to miss Vernon's picnic."

Every May, Vernon and Helena, Lord and Lady West, invited family and friends to this extravagant open-air gathering. Morwenna wasn't sure what had started the tradition. It wasn't anyone's birthday, and when she'd asked if the date marked some anniversary, her brother-in-law smiled at his striking wife and didn't answer.

Today the weather was perfect. Through some alchemy, it usually was, although once or twice they'd had to retreat to the Wests' elegant house in Mayfair. Morwenna looked around at a scene that could have graced a medieval tournament. Flower-bedecked tents and pavilions, bowers of cushions and divans, tables groaning with food and wine. And for the guests' entertainment, horses, gigs, dogs, boats, a maypole, archery butts, and a string quartet, doing their best to be heard above the shrieks and laughter of a crowd of overexcited children.

"I haven't seen the Kinglakes since Christmas." Sally and Charles had stayed at Belleville for a couple of weeks over the Festive Season. Morwenna had worried that her stylish, fastidious friends might find her rambunctious family too much to handle en masse, but it had turned out to be a happy reunion. She and Robert rarely came to London, and even when they did, Sally and Charles were often away traveling.

How she loved her life on the beautiful and now prosperous estate that Robert had bought from Silas seven years ago. Seven eventful years for the family, as a quick check around the field proved.

Silas and Caro were here with their four children, their oldest Roberta now fourteen and growing into a beauty like her mother. Traces of gray showed in Silas's thick tawny hair, while Caro glowed with the contentment of a life well lived. Helena and Vernon, of course, with their three children. Fenella and Anthony Townsend had brought their son and daughter, Henry and Emily, while their older boys, Carey Townsend and Brandon Deerham, had come along to help keep the boisterous youngsters under control.

The first three Dashing Widows had found love and fulfillment, and paved the way for the second trio of Dashing Widows to make their way to happiness.

Morwenna was certainly happy with how everything had worked out. Robert had wanted a big family, and fate had delivered one. Her sons, seven-year-old Michael and six-year-old Frederick, both lean and dark like their father, were playing around the boats along the riverbank. Robert's fascination with sailing had continued into the next generation.

Her daughters Kate and Bella trailed their older sister Kerenza about the field, no doubt driving her mad. At twelve, Kerenza had to cope with endless adoration from the little girls of three and four, although most of the time, she took it in her stride. Kerenza, Morwenna was pleased to say, took most things in her stride.

She stared down at Anne, six months old, and already promising to be another child who wasn't too fussed about unimportant things.

A bark caught her attention. Kerenza had stopped

to lift Kate onto a fat piebald pony, while Bella played with Kerenza's dog Rascal. Rascal more than lived up to his name. Morwenna often wished they'd called the black spaniel Little Angel.

"Goodness me, you're so dreamy at the moment. It's hardly worth trying to talk to you," Amy said crossly. "Did you hear me say the news is all over Town that the King is ill? It looks like we might have a queen on the throne before the end of the year."

"That's nice," Morwenna said, although she hardly cared. Her days as part of London society seemed long ago now.

Amy sighed impatiently. "I'm sure I wasn't nearly so besotted with my babies."

That caught Morwenna's attention. "I'm sure you were—and are."

Amy had borne her first child, golden-haired Charlotte, five months after Robert came home. Wilfred arrived two years later. The strikingly good-looking Dacre children were hanging around their cousins on the riverbank, under the watchful eye of Miss Carroll and their father Gervaise, Lord Pascal.

These days, Amy and Pascal didn't spend much more time in Town than Morwenna and Robert. London's handsomest man had, much to the fashionable world's astonishment, become a dedicated farmer. He and his wife devoted most of their attention to a thriving estate in Shropshire, where Amy received great acclaim for her experiments in cattle breeding.

"Who knew I'd find my children even more interesting than my prize Herefords?" Amy paused to admire the sleeping baby. "You're so lucky that Anne is such a quiet child. Both of mine howled like banshees for the first two years."

Morwenna smiled down at her daughter, loving her pink cheeks and soft, light brown curls. She was going to grow up to be one of the leonine Nashes. "After Bella, I deserve a quiet baby. I swear she didn't sleep a wink until she was three."

"She's still a bundle of energy," Amy said, glancing across to where Bella rushed over to torment her cousin Wilfred, Amy's dark-haired son.

Sally and Charles, both as always dressed in the first stare of fashion, approached them up the hill. Once the flurry of greetings was over, Sally was holding Anne, and Charles had gone in search of Silas who was, as usual at these picnics, talking horses with their host.

"Isn't she beautiful?" Sally said softly, running an elegant finger down the baby's rounded cheek.

"Well, I think so." From habit, Morwenna searched her friend's face for some sign of regret or resentment that she'd never had children. But Sally and Charles were so wrapped up in each other, she supposed they were happy as they were. "She's grown since you last saw her."

The Kinglakes had made Anne's acquaintance last Christmas, not long after she arrived in the world. Sally lowered her voice, although only Amy and

Morwenna were within earshot. "We're not telling anyone yet, just in case, but…"

Amy's face lit up with joy. "Sally, are you going to have a baby?"

Eyes bright with tears, Sally nodded. "In October, if all goes well."

"Charles will be overjoyed."

Sally accepted Morwenna's handkerchief and balancing Anne on one arm, wiped her eyes. "He's pleased and worried in equal measure—I'm thirty-nine after all. But the doctors say I'm as healthy as a horse. And I feel marvelous."

"Oh, Sally, I'm so happy for you." Morwenna laid her hand on Sally's arm.

"How are my favorite girls getting on?" Robert said from behind her.

"Why, thank you, kind sir," Sally said, turning and batting her eyelashes at him.

"Of course you're my favorite," he said, kissing her cheek and taking his newest daughter into his arms. Anne opened bright hazel eyes and gave a satisfied murmur at the move. She adored her papa beyond anything in the world, except perhaps Rascal.

"What about me?" Amy asked.

"You're all my favorites." Robert smiled at his sister. "Don't you know that?"

These days, Robert smiled a lot, and a large gathering like this presented no difficulties. He was no longer the troubled, damaged man who had come back to Morwenna almost eight years ago. Even the horrific slash on his face had faded to a subtle silver. In her opinion, the scar made him look rather dashing.

It had been nearly a year before he told her the full story of his captivity in South America, and she still occasionally woke from nightmares inspired by the horrors he'd described. But that long, sleepless night when he'd relived every harrowing detail for her had been like lancing a wound. Since then, he'd risen above his ordeal with a courage that awed her.

"Good try, brother," Amy said without rancor.

"You're definitely my favorite youngest sister." He tilted his chin toward the activity down in the field. "I believe the races are about to start."

Contests of horsemanship always formed part of the picnic's entertainment. Morwenna watched Silas and Vernon, still best friends, still competitive, mount up. Pascal was already sitting on his chestnut mare, although with Vernon riding last year's Derby champion, he didn't stand a chance of winning. But that hardly mattered when a man looked as spectacular in the saddle as he did.

Everyone, adults and children, started to move toward the makeshift course to watch the fun. All except Morwenna and Robert who lingered behind on the rise with their new daughter. Amy was right. Morwenna was besotted. And so, she was delighted to note, was Anne's papa.

"Anthony's playing umpire again," Robert said,

frowning into the sun. At the finish line, Anthony Townsend, Lord Kenwick, towered over his delicate blond wife Fenella.

"At least he's big enough to stop any fights," Morwenna said with a fond laugh.

"Not that he gets much practice with his perfect wife and perfect children," Robert said wryly. "He should come and pour oil on troubled waters at my house. That would really test his skills."

Morwenna cast him a sardonic glance. "Your children are perfect."

He rolled his eyes. "When they're asleep. Maybe."

"You wouldn't have it any other way."

He shook his dark head. "No, I love their spirit. They get it from their mother."

She arched her eyebrows. "Are you saying she's not perfect either?"

His smile held such a wealth of unconditional love, her breath caught. "She's perfect for me."

"Oh, Robert..." Even after all these years, he maintained the ability to turn her heart to syrup.

He leaned in, juggling the baby, and kissed her. "I love you, my darling."

"And I love you." She blinked away the misty haze in front of her eyes. "We've been lucky, haven't we?"

They had, despite their years of heartbreak and separation. Robert had needed a long time to recover from his captivity and find his way on land instead of on the water, but they had made a good life in Devon.

And Morwenna could never doubt how much he loved his family. And her. "Yes, we've been blessed."

Holding Anne with one powerful arm, Robert slung the other around his wife's shoulders. As Helena called "go" to start 1837's Dashing Widows Cup, Morwenna leaned against her husband in perfect contentment. She barely spared a glance for the riders down in the field.

As far as she was concerned, it didn't matter a fig who won the Dashing Widows Cup today. What mattered was that in the game of life, all the Dashing Widows had emerged victorious.

ABOUT THE AUTHOR

ANNA CAMPBELL has written 10 multi award-winning historical romances for Grand Central Publishing and Avon HarperCollins, and her work is published in 22 languages. She has also written 21 bestselling independently published romances, including her series, The Dashing Widows and The Lairds Most Likely. Anna has won numerous awards for her Regency-set stories including Romantic Times Reviewers Choice, the Booksellers Best, the Golden Quill (three times), the Heart of Excellence (twice), the Write Touch, the Aspen Gold (twice) and the Australian Romance Readers Association's favorite historical romance (five times). Her books have three times been nominated for Romance Writers of America's prestigious RITA Award, and three times for Australia's Romantic Book of the Year. When she's not traveling the world seeking inspiration for her stories, Anna lives on the beautiful east coast of Australia.

Anna loves to hear from her readers. You can find her at:

Website: www.annacampbell.com

facebook.com/AnnaCampbellFans

twitter.com/AnnaCampbellOz

bookbub.com/authors/anna-campbell

goodreads.com/AnnaCampbell

ALSO BY ANNA CAMPBELL

Claiming the Courtesan

Untouched

Tempt the Devil

Captive of Sin

My Reckless Surrender

Midnight's Wild Passion

The Sons of Sin series:

Seven Nights in a Rogue's Bed

Days of Rakes and Roses

A Rake's Midnight Kiss

What a Duke Dares

A Scoundrel by Moonlight

Three Proposals and a Scandal

The Dashing Widows:

The Seduction of Lord Stone

Tempting Mr. Townsend

Winning Lord West

Pursuing Lord Pascal

Charming Sir Charles

Catching Captain Nash

Lord Garson's Bride

The Lairds Most Likely:

The Laird's Willful Lass

The Laird's Christmas Kiss

The Highlander's Lost Lady

Christmas Stories:

The Winter Wife

Her Christmas Earl

A Pirate for Christmas

Mistletoe and the Major

A Match Made in Mistletoe

The Christmas Stranger

Other Books:

These Haunted Hearts

Stranded with the Scottish Earl

THE SEDUCTION OF LORD STONE

(The Dashing Widows Book 1)

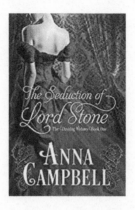

For this reckless widow, love is the most dangerous game of all.

Caroline, Lady Beaumont, arrives in London seeking excitement after ten dreary years of marriage and an even drearier year of mourning. That means conquering society, dancing like there's no tomorrow, and taking a lover to provide passion without promises. Promises, in this dashing widow's dictionary, equal prison. So what is an adventurous lady to do when she loses her heart to a notorious rake who, for the first time in his life, wants forever?

Devilish Silas Nash, Viscount Stone is in love at last with a beautiful, headstrong widow bent on playing the field. Worse, she's enlisted his help to set her up with his disreputable best friend. No red-blooded man takes such a challenge lying down, and Silas schemes to seduce his darling into his arms, warm, willing and besotted. But will his passionate plots come undone against a woman determined to act the mistress, but never the wife?

TEMPTING MR TOWNSEND

(The Dashing Widows Book 2)

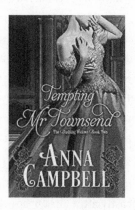

Beauty...

Fenella, Lady Deerham has rejoined society after five years of mourning her beloved husband's death at Waterloo. Now she's fêted as a diamond of the first water and London's perfect lady. But beneath her exquisite exterior, this delicate blond beauty conceals depths of courage and passion nobody has ever suspected. When her son and his school friend go missing, she vows to find them whatever it takes. Including setting off alone in the middle of the night with high-handed bear of a man, Anthony Townsend.

Will this tumultuous journey end in more tragedy? Or will the impetuous quest astonish this Dashing Widow with a breathtaking new love, and life with the last man she ever imagined?

And the Beast?

When Anthony Townsend bursts into Lady Deerham's fashionable Mayfair mansion demanding the return of his orphaned nephew, the lovely widow's beauty and spirit turn his world upside down. But surely such a refined and aristocratic creature will scorn a rough, self-made man's courtship, even if that man is now one of the richest magnates in England. Especially after he's made such a woeful first impression by barging into her house and accusing her of conniving with the runaways. But when Fenella insists on sharing the desperate search for the boys, fate offers Anthony a chance to play the hero and change her mind about him.

Will reluctant proximity convince Fenella that perhaps Mr. Townsend isn't so beastly after all? Or now that their charges are safe, will Anthony and Fenella remain forever opposites fighting their attraction?

WINNING LORD WEST

(The Dashing Widows Book 3)

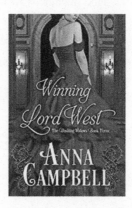

All rakes are the same! Except when they're not...

Spirited Helena, Countess of Crewe, knows all about profligate rakes; she was married to one for nine years and still bears the scars. Now this Dashing Widow plans a life of glorious freedom where she does just what she wishes – and nobody will ever hurt her again.

So what is she to do when that handsome scoundrel Lord West sets out to make her his wife? Say no, of course. Which is fine, until West focuses all his sensual skills on changing her mind. And West's sensual skills are renowned far and wide as utterly irresistible...

Passionate persuasion!

Vernon Grange, Lord West, has long been estranged from his headstrong first love, Helena Nash, but he's always regretted that he didn't step in to prevent her disastrous marriage.

Now Helena is free, and this time, come hell or high water, West won't let her escape him again.

His weapon of choice is seduction, and in this particular game, he's an acknowledged master. Now that he and Helena are under one roof at the year's most glamorous house party, he intends to counter her every argument with breathtaking pleasure. Could it be that Lady Crewe's dashing days are numbered?

PURSUING LORD PASCAL

(The Dashing Widows Book 4)

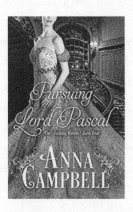

Golden Days...

Famous for her agricultural innovations, Amy, Lady
Mowbray has never had a romantical thought in her life.
Well, apart from her short-lived crush on London's
handsomest man, Lord Pascal, when she was a brainless 14-
year-old. She even chose her late husband because he owned
the best herd of beef cattle in England!

But fate steps in and waltzes this practical widow out of her
rustic retreat into the glamour of the London season. When
Pascal pursues her, all her adolescent fantasies come true.
Those fantasies turn disturbingly adult when grown-up
desire enters the equation. Amy plunges headlong into a
reckless affair that promises pleasure beyond her wildest
dreams – until she discovers that this glittering world hides
damaging secrets and painful revelations set to break a
country girl's tender heart.

All that glitters...

Gervaise Dacre, Lord Pascal needs to marry money to save his estate, devastated after a violent storm. He's never much liked his reputation as London's handsomest man, but it certainly comes in handy when the time arrives to seek a rich bride. Unfortunately, the current crop of debutantes bores him silly, and he finds himself praying for a sensible woman with a generous dowry.

When he meets Dashing Widow Amy Mowbray, it seems all his prayers have been answered. Until he finds himself in thrall to the lovely widow, and his mercenary quest becomes dangerously complicated. Soon he's much more interested in passion than in pounds, shillings and pence. What happens if Amy discovers the sordid truth behind his whirlwind courtship? And if she does, will she see beyond his original, selfish motives to the ardent love that lies unspoken in his sinful heart?

CHARMING SIR CHARLES

(The Dashing Widows Book 5)

Matchmaking mayhem in Mayfair!

Sally Cowan, Countess of Norwood, spent ten miserable
years married to an overbearing oaf. Now she's free, she
plans to have some fun. But before she kicks her heels up,
this Dashing Widow sets out to launch her pretty,
headstrong niece Meg into society and find her a good
husband.

When rich and charming Sir Charles Kinglake gives every
sign that he can't get enough of Meg's company, Sally is
delighted to play chaperone at all their meetings. Charles is
everything that's desirable in a gentleman suitor. How
disastrous, when over the course of the season's most elegant
house party, Sally realizes that desire is precisely the name of
the game. She's found her niece's perfect match—but she
wants him for herself!

There are none so blind as those who will not see...

From the moment Sir Charles Kinglake meets sparkling Lady Norwood, he's smitten. He courts her as a gentleman should—dancing with her at every glittering ball, taking her to the theatre, escorting her around London. Because she's acting as chaperone to her niece, that means most times, Meg accompanies them. The lack of privacy chafes a man consumed by desire, but Charles's intentions are honorable, and he's willing to work within the rules to win the wife he wants.

However when he discovers that his careful pursuit has convinced Sally he's interested in Meg rather than her, he flings the rules out the window. When love is at stake, who cares about a little scandal? It's time for charming Sir Charles to abandon the subtle approach and play the passionate lover, not the society suitor!

Now with everything at sixes and sevens, Sir Charles risks everything to show lovely Lady Norwood they make the perfect pair!

LORD GARSON'S BRIDE

(The Dashing Widows Book 7)

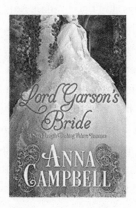

Lord Garson's dilemma.

Hugh Rutherford, Lord Garson, loved and lost when his
fiancée returned to the husband she'd believed drowned. In
the three years since, Garson has come to loathe his
notoriety as London's most famous rejected suitor. It's high
time to find a bride, a level-headed, well-bred lady who will
accept a loveless marriage and cause no trouble. Luckily he
has just the candidate in mind.

A marriage of convenience...

When Lady Jane Norris receives an unexpected proposal
from her childhood friend Lord Garson, marriage to the
handsome baron rescues her from a grim future. At twenty-
eight, Jane is on the shelf and under no illusions about her
attractions. With her father's death, she's lost her home and
faces life as an impecunious spinster. While she's aware

Garson will never love again, they have friendship and goodwill to build upon. What can possibly go wrong?

...becomes very inconvenient indeed.

From the first, things don't go to plan, not least because Garson soon finds himself in thrall to his surprisingly intriguing bride. A union grounded in duty veers toward obsession. And when the Dashing Widows take Jane in hand and transform her into the toast of London, Garson isn't the only man to notice his wife's beauty and charm. He's known Jane all her life, but suddenly she's a dazzling stranger. This isn't the uncomplicated, pragmatic match he signed up for. When Jane defies the final taboo and asks for his love, her impossible demand threatens to blast this convenient marriage to oblivion.

Once the dust settles, will Lord Garson still be the man who can only love once?

Made in the USA
Coppell, TX
20 August 2020